The Asking Price

Books by Henry Cecil

Fiction

THE ASKING PRICE
A CHILD DIVIDED
PORTRAIT OF A JUDGE AND OTHER STORIES
DAUGHTERS IN LAW
SETTLED OUT OF COURT
SOBER AS A JUDGE
THE LONG ARM
FRIENDS AT COURT
BROTHERS IN LAW
ACCORDING TO THE EVIDENCE
NO BAIL FOR THE JUDGE

Nonfiction

BRIEF TO COUNSEL

HENRY CECIL

The Asking Price

HARPER & ROW, PUBLISHERS

New York

LIBRARY OF CONGRESS CATALOG CARD NUMBER: 66–21715

G-Q

The Asking Price

1

❀

For Sale

MR. HIGHCASTLE, OF HIGHCASTLE AND NEWBURY, surveyors and estate agents, sighed faintly. It was a very professional sigh. He had learned it from his father, who had been a pawnbroker. In his father's case it had been intended to convey that, if the stones really were diamonds, the ring wouldn't be worth all that much and that anyway money was in short supply. It would be followed by:

"Lend you ten pounds, buy it for fifteen."

"But another place told me it was worth fifty."

"Remember the address?" his father would ask.

"Certainly, it's—"

"Well, as you remember it," his father would interrupt, "I should go there, if I were you."

The lender's sigh had been successfully passed on to the estate agent.

"So you want to sell your house," said Mr. Highcastle. "Please sit down."

The customer sat.

"May I have your full name, please?"

1

"Ronald Timothy Holbrook."

"And your address, Mr. Holbrook?"

"It's Colonel, as a matter of fact."

"Sorry, Colonel."

"I wouldn't have mentioned it," said Ronald Holbrook, "but I thought it sometimes helped. In the advertisements, you know."

"Ah," said Mr. Highcastle, "you mean something of this sort: 'Axed colonel, never actually court-martialed, wishes to sell his detention barracks, which could be converted into a most attractive penthouse (now out of fashion) at exorbitant expense. It would be absurd to pay ten thousand pounds for it. Try an offer.'"

"Not bad," said Ronald admiringly.

"Thank you," said Mr. Highcastle. "I don't actually use that type of advertisement myself. I hate giving something for nothing if I can help it."

"How d'you mean?"

"Well, we poor agents are doing it all the time, you know. Hours and hours of work trying to sell a house, and then the client decides not to sell. And we don't get a penny. So it goes against the grain to give additional reading matter to the newspapers for nothing. I believe some people buy the better Sunday newspapers simply to read Mr. Brooks's advertisements. And now your address, please, Colonel."

"Well, in confidence, it's Eighteen Eleanor Gardens, Islington."

"Islington?" queried Mr. Highcastle. "You mean Canonbury?"

"We always call it Islington."

"Well, we don't," said Mr. Highcastle. "Eighteen Eleanor Gardens, Canonbury," he said as he wrote it down.

"You will keep it confidential, won't you?"

"You can rely on us, Colonel. And what price are you asking?"

"I'd like to get ten thousand pounds."

A cough was substituted for a sigh.

"I'm sure you would, Colonel. So would a lot of people."

"But there's a great shortage of houses, isn't there?"

"There may be," said Mr. Highcastle, "but there is a greater shortage of buyers. And, quite frankly, this type of house is very difficult to sell. I won't say it's a drag on the market. That would be going too far. But there's no money, you see. Now, flats, or very small houses, are a different matter. They're snapped up at once. But seven- or eight-room houses are very difficult. I might get you five or six thousand."

"Five or six!" said Ronald, and his voice showed horror at the suggestion. "But I've read of houses like this being sold for ten or eleven thousand."

"D'you happen to know the name of the agents who sold them?"

"I don't, as a matter of fact."

"Pity," said Mr. Highcastle. "I'd have suggested your going to them."

Mr. Highcastle's father would have approved.

"What's the most you think I can get?"

"I suggest eight thousand pounds as an asking price, but I'd strongly advise you to take six."

"I couldn't possibly accept so little."

"Just as you say, Colonel. But I'm sure you'll understand that we're in this together. It's to our mutual interest to get as much as possible. The more you get, the more we get."

"Well, please do the best you can," said Ronald.

"We always do."

"And your definite view is that houses of this size in London are not fetching good prices?"

"That is not just my view, Colonel. It is a fact. You can't argue with facts. Most purchasers of this type of house need a mortgage. Is yours mortgaged, by the way, Colonel?"

"As a matter of fact, it is not."

"Well, that makes no difference in the case of a sale. But it's a great advantage these days to have cash when you're buying a house. But how many people have the cash? Nothing like enough. And nowadays mortgages are very difficult. You've got to be young or youngish, healthy, and earning a good salary. And even then you may not get one."

"Well, you've cheered me up in one way," said Ronald. "I want to buy a house in London. Not a very small house or flat, but a seven- or eight-room house with the usual and I don't mind if one of the rooms on the upper floor is divided into two or not. In other words, the type of house which you assured me was almost a drag on the market. I'm glad to hear that it should be easy to get and won't cost much. And I don't need a mortgage."

If Mr. Highcastle felt in the least embarrassed, his professional experience enabled him not to show it in the least.

"In what particular neighborhood?" he asked blandly.

"Anywhere," said Ronald, "which is nowhere near Islington—I mean Canonbury."

"Have you any particular requirement?" went on Mr. Highcastle.

"No," said Ronald. "Something like what I've got now, but I'm not particular, except that it must be away from Canonbury."

"And what sort of price have you in mind? Ten or twelve thousand?"

"Good gracious no. Something less than I shall get for mine."

Mr. Highcastle sighed.

"I'm afraid that won't be at all easy."

"But you just said that these houses were difficult to sell."

"Indeed they are. But I didn't say they were easy to buy. Sellers are holding back. Waiting for an improvement."

"Then you would recommend me not to sell mine yet?"

"On the contrary, Colonel. I would recommend you to sell before things get worse."

"But you said that sellers are holding back, waiting for an improvement."

"I did indeed, but I didn't say that they were right to do so. In my considered opinion they're in for a nasty shock. In a year's time your house may fetch even less than it would today."

"Then why can't I buy from someone like myself?"

"Because people are very stupid, Colonel, and—I'm sorry to have to say it—greedy. Of course, some people like yourself, Colonel, may be forced to sell because they need the money. Forgive me for mentioning it, Colonel."

"There's no need to apologize. I'm not ashamed of wanting money. Other people want it too. Surely there must be other people owning a house like mine who have to sell it?"

"I'm sure there are, Colonel."

"Then why can't I buy one of their houses?"

"Quite simply, Colonel, because there aren't enough of them.

Their houses are snapped up as soon as they come on the market."

"Then why isn't mine?"

"Because your price is too high, Colonel. I could sell yours tomorrow for—for forty-five hundred pounds."

"I daresay. No doubt you could. No doubt someone would accept it as a gift."

"What is the state of repair, may I ask?" said Mr. Highcastle, of whom his father would have become prouder and prouder during this conversation. "I should have asked you before. My suggested prices were, of course, based on it being in a good state of repair."

"It's in very fair repair."

"No woodworm, or dry rot?"

"Certainly not."

"You've had it examined, then?"

"Why should I?"

"Then how can you know for certain, Colonel? I'm afraid there are more infested houses than you think. Have you a cellar?"

"Yes."

"A frequent source of trouble. What about the roof timbers?"

"I've never been in the loft."

"Let's hope it's all right," said Mr. Highcastle. "But I can assure you that some houses are so pest-ridden that they're worth little more than the site value. Not that, sometimes."

"So the long and the short of it is this," said Ronald. "No one wants a house like mine, so I shall only get a low price for it. On the other hand, no one will sell houses like mine, because the prices are too low. It's a buyer's market for my house, but a seller's for every other house of the same description. In addition to that, my house is lucky to be standing at all and, if I don't get prosecuted by the local council for having a dangerous structure, I shall be lucky."

"I take it," said Mr. Highcastle, "that you would like to take your business elsewhere?"

"Not at all," said Ronald. "Hurry up with both houses as quickly as you can. I've got to get out."

2

The Vender

RONALD WAS FIFTY-TWO and he had lived in Islington for nearly twenty years. He was one of the first objects of interest which new residents usually discovered, for his great asset in life was his aptitude for personal relationships. Everyone liked him and women sometimes adored him. He was excessively lazy, had no regard for the truth and was a persistent and unashamed borrower. But he borrowed so charmingly it was difficult to resist him. His "I suppose you couldn't by any chance lend me . . . ?" was irresistible to most people. He never deliberately cheated anyone, though, had it been essential to do so, he would have yielded to the inevitable without any trouble from his conscience. He could fairly have been described as a parasite, but for the fact that he made a definite contribution to the world merely by existing. Anyone who could instill happiness into his neighbor by borrowing a lawn-mower or a pound of sugar does, at least to some extent, pull his weight. The fact that it involves no conscious effort on the part of the borrower does not detract from the benefit it confers. There is not all that happiness on earth that one can afford to dispense with people who add to the store of it. He had quite a good intelligence but was far too idle to make use of it, except in extremities.

So, if the inhabitants of the world had been suddenly assembled and ordered from on High to be decimated on merit, it would have been most unlikely that Ronald would have been extinguished. At first sight he would have been an obvious case. He belonged to no profession, he had no job, no business, he contributed nothing tangible to the public store, except for rates and taxes, he had not even produced sons and daughters and, though still capable of doing so, showed no sign whatever of getting started. And, indeed, any progeny of his might have inherited only the laziness and none of the charm. Nevertheless, when the Recording Angel read out the names and called for justification for continued existence, Ronald, probably arriving late, would have charmed the Angel from the start.

"You're late."

"I'm terribly sorry. I'm afraid I usually am."

"But this is a special occasion."

"I know. That makes it so much worse."

Ronald would have adopted the same attitude he adopted over motorcar accidents. He nearly always softened the other driver, who rushed up to him breathing fire and slaughter, by apologizing profusely and sometimes adding:

"I'm always doing this, I'm afraid."

"Then you ought to be off the road."

"I know," Ronald would say. "D'you think we should report it to the police?"

Only once had an angry driver said "yes" and proceeded with Ronald to the nearest police station.

"Anyone hurt?" asked the sergeant.

"No."

"Doesn't concern us," said the sergeant, and turned his attention to a lady who had lost her dog. It is not surprising that motorists are not deterred from selfish driving by the fear of penalties. There are not enough police to observe anything like one percent of the cases which occur, and normally, where there are no personal injuries, the police refuse to prosecute unless they have seen the incident themselves. And it is curious how often a policeman's back is turned to a slight accident. Death or grave personal injury may have been a few inches off but, as long as it was only a possibility, and there was no actual injury, the police seldom take any interest, unless they have personally seen a breach of the traffic regulations.

The old motoring story of the police and the driver of the fast car could well have been told of Ronald. A police car trailed a high-powered car, and the policemen were surprised to find that, though the driver went very fast on unrestricted parts of the road, he observed every speed limit and altogether gave a perfect example of good driving. The two policemen decided to congratulate the driver. Accordingly they passed him and signaled him to stop. He obeyed their signals and the police car stopped in front of him. The policemen walked back to the high-powered car.

"It's all right, sir," said one of them to the driver, when he saw the anxious look he gave them. "You've done nothing wrong at all. On the contrary, we want to congratulate you on the extreme care you have taken, in spite of the power of your car. Well done, sir."

The driver did not speak for a moment and then slowly he said:

"It's like this, officer. When you're as tight as I am, you've got to be careful."

It would have taken a very hardhearted policeman to arrest such a driver.

The Recording Angel would have been far more likely to put on the short list for extinction the lady in the post office who was never late for work, seldom away through illness, did her full stint every day, was never in trouble of any kind, but who had never been known to smile at the customer when she sold a stamp, and would often keep people waiting for no obvious reason without an apology. Without such ladies the post office could not carry on. Without similar people in all branches of the state machinery, civilian life would grind to a halt. Ronald's absence would have made no practical difference to the world. But he would have been sadly missed by many people outside his immediate family, while the post-office lady would not. And she could easily have been replaced. But not Ronald.

It would not, of course, do if the world were composed of

Ronalds, but a few of them dotted around are definite assets.

Before the Second World War, Ronald had been a civil servant in an undistinguished position. He had been educated at a public school and Oxford, but those were the days when hard work was not necessary. He had just got through his examinations and was eventually called to the bar. But there he found that not only was hard work essential but that it was often unrewarded. He had actually worked really hard on a case once. He had been asked to do it at the last moment by another barrister. He worked right through the night and was actually successful the next day. But he was not paid a penny and only received the most casual thanks for what he had done. His humor was not improved when his clerk told him that it was excellent experience, and he soon decided that it was not the sort of experience he wanted to repeat.

He left the bar and drifted into the civil service, but there he found even the irregular hours which he kept far too regular, and, though in order to live he had to remain on for some years, he was almost glad when the war came and he went into the Army. There he did quite a useful job in an infantry battalion—not because of his military proficiency, which was negligible, but because everyone liked him. He was definitely a morale-raiser, and his death would have been far more lamented than that of the extremely efficient but equally bloody antitank-platoon commander. Ronald's only assets were his cheerfulness, friendliness, and the fact that he never panicked. He had no eye for country and no head for administration. He made some sort of effort to carry out the orders which he was given, but not very successfully, while the orders which he gave, if intelligible at all, were usually almost incapable of being carried out. He never rose above the rank of lieutenant. Had he not been Ronald, he would have lost his commission early in the war. But each successive battalion commander went through the same phases regarding him. At first the CO would say to himself, "That's a charming fellow. Glad I've got him." Very soon afterward, having discovered his extreme indolence, he would say, "I must get rid of this chap." And then, as it takes a little time to get rid of this chap, he would suddenly become aware of the advantage there was in having Ronald about the place. So that is how he was used. To be about the place. And, in and out of danger, officers and men were glad that he was there. He might not be able to make the simplest plan successfully, but his mere presence was an asset.

"Go on, Private Hemmings," he would say to the battalion joker during a particularly unpleasant bombardment of his platoon's position, "go on, make me laugh."

Providence decreed that Ronald should be neither killed nor wounded, and he was the only officer in his battalion who went right through from Dunkirk to Berlin. His last CO recommended him for a mention in dispatches. But the brigadier queried it.

"That fellow?" he said. "All he seems to do is smile."

"True enough," said Ronald's CO. "But we've found it a pretty useful smile."

"Well, I'm afraid I've no sense of humor," said the brigadier, which was true, though he did not mean it. "Put up someone else."

So Ronald left the Army with nothing but a host of friends and his rank of lieutenant. And then he had a piece of luck. It was at the time when temporary civil servants in the Ministry of Supply— most of whom would never have been employed but for the war— had discovered a lucrative method of disposing of surplus stores. Ronald managed to get in on a deal involving a vast quantity of parachute silk. In the end he found himself the richer by £60,000. It was the best day in his life. The horrible fear that he might have to work again for his living vanished. Somehow or other he could live forever on £60,000. He promoted himself to colonel and bought a house in Islington.

3

❋

Eleanor Gardens

THERE WERE TWENTY-FIVE HOUSES in Eleanor Gardens. A few of them had been converted into flats, but most of them were still private houses when Ronald bought his. He had described it correctly to Mr. Highcastle and the same description would have been true of nearly all the other houses. Most of them were ugly late-Victorian houses, but solidly built. By the time Ronald wanted to sell No. 18, most of them were inhabited by professionals or well-to-do businessmen.

There were two barristers, who, unusually for the legal profession, disliked each other intensely. Whether it is due to the small number of practicing barristers or to some other reason, the fact is there is very little enmity or unpleasant rivalry among members of the bar. There are, of course, a few petty jealousies and an occasional example of the situation which existed between the two who lived in Eleanor Gardens, but for the most part barristers, however competitive the situation may be between them and their fellows, are friendly and helpful toward each other. It is, therefore, a very happy profession. Cynical laymen might say that, as there are only two thousand of them battening on the frailties of their fellowmen, they can afford to smile at each other.

That was certainly the view of one of Ronald's neighbors, George Hazelgrove, a businessman whose only interest was his work. He had been involved in disastrous litigation, although six judges decided in his favor and only three against him. It was a case about a patent. The judge who tried the case decided in his favor. Three judges in the Court of Appeal dismissed his opponent's appeal. But the House of Lords by a majority of three to two decided against him. The case cost George Hazelgrove's company some £20,000 directly and a good deal more indirectly. He never went to law again and, though he did not personally dislike either of the two barristers who were his neighbors, he always found it slightly embarrassing to be in their company, as he could not forget that they were the associates of a profession which had caused him punishing loss.

Eleanor Gardens contained one practical joker—not a man like the famous Cole, who received a degree at a university as the Sultan of Zanzibar, took up part of Piccadilly and conducted other similar experiments. Andrew Melrose's jokes were less spectacular and less physical, but they could be decidedly embarrassing to people. In his professional life of a stockbroker he indulged in no hoaxes. He reserved that for his neighbors.

Mrs. Vintage, the elderly widow at No. 8, was said to be fabulously wealthy, and indeed her mode of life was strong evidence of the truth of this belief. She had three domestic servants, a chauffeur and a Rolls-Royce. She said little but no one could be sure if she thought much. Her smile showed that she intended to be friendly but her conversation was mainly monosyllabic.

"Good morning, Mrs. Vintage. Barbara and I were wondering if you could dine with us one day before you went."

"Please."

"We shan't be dressing up."

"Oh?"

The old lady was plainly disappointed.

"Unless you'd prefer it."

"Yes, please."

"Of course. We'll put on all our finery."

Mrs. Vintage condescended to a whole sentence. She must have felt strongly on the subject.

"When I was a girl," she said, "one either dined out or one did not."

"We'll make it a party. How about Tuesday week? At eight."

Mrs. Vintage nodded.

"Thank you. At eight."

She was sitting in her car during this conversation.

"Dawkins," she said, "drive."

And Dawkins drove.

If the wealthiest person in Eleanor Gardens was Mrs. Vintage, the most distinguished was certainly the former High Court Judge Sir William Venables. Ronald had first known him as a successful barrister. Then he became a judge and, after fifteen years on the bench, he retired. He was well within the age limit, but he had always looked forward to having a few years to himself when he could do what he liked when he liked. But he soon found after retirement that reading and grandchildren were not enough. He started to write for the newspapers and even to appear on television. He was a moderate after-dinner speaker and was invited to functions when no better speaker was available or sometimes, very deferentially, at short notice when the original speaker and the two reserves had been struck down with influenza. He enjoyed these occasions and only refused if he was genuinely unable to go.

Sir William had been a popular judge because he was always friendly, but his decisions were often set aside on appeal and he was, on the whole, a poor judge of character.

The legal profession did not have it all its own way in Eleanor Gardens, even though there was a solicitor as well. There were three accountants and two surveyors, an architect and an engineer, and one householder who worked very late at night but whose profession or business no one knew. The light in his study would be seen burning nearly every night and, as the blinds and curtains were not drawn, he could be seen at a desk writing or apparently pondering some problem. He was the only mystery in the Gardens, and when conversation at dinner flagged it was a commonplace to speculate on what Mr. Sinclair did. He did not encourage conversation, though he was polite enough if anyone said "Good morning" or asked the time. He always repelled any attempts to find out more about him. When he first came to Eleanor Gardens, a few years after Ronald, many of the residents had tried to get this information from him.

"Saw you working very late last night, Mr. Sinclair."

"Maybe I was," replied Sinclair, in a slight Scottish accent.

"And it's not the first time. You must work very hard."

"Aye, I do."

"Don't you get tired sometimes?"

"Aye, I do."

"Would it be impertinent of me to ask you what you're working at?"

"Aye, it would."

"I'm so sorry. I meant no offense."

"No offense taken."

Even Mrs. Vintage had broken out of her monosyllables in an effort to lift the veil on Mr. Sinclair.

"Now you really must tell me what you do," she had once said.

"I must, must I, Mrs. Vintage?"

"Yes, you really must."

"Must is a strong word. Why must I?"

"I'm a woman, and inquisitive."

"Ye'll have to give me a better reason than that."

"I want to know."

"There are many things we want to know but never find out."

Mrs. Vintage gave up.

"Drive, Dawkins," she said.

But it was not the mysterious Sinclair or the lawyers in Eleanor Gardens or Mrs. Vintage or the accountants and surveyor nor yet the disappointed litigant Hazelgrove who provided the reason for Ronald wanting to get out. That reason lived in No. 19, next door to him.

4

Number Nineteen

SHE WAS SEVENTEEN. Ronald had heard her being born, seen her christened and confirmed, watched her grow from nothing upward. Ronald was a bachelor. He was fond of women and had had a number of affairs but either marriage had eluded him or he had eluded marriage. He himself was never quite certain which. Sometimes, when feeling a little maudlin after a good dinner, he would confide to his attractive companion that he had once fallen in love with the wife of a friend of his.

"Well, it's a thing one can't do, isn't it?" he would say rather like a distinguished airman half-apologizing for a couple of DSO's and a DFC. "Well, one can't actually run away, can one?"

"A lot of people would," his companion would say. "It's nice to meet someone so unselfish. It must have been terrible for you."

"I've managed, you know," said Ronald, conveying in that short sentence that his virtuous behavior had resulted in a blighted life, which somehow or other he managed to live through. "But it's good to meet someone so understanding. Even some of my best friends told me that I was mad not to run off with Tania—now I've told you her name. I shouldn't have done that. Please forget it. Normally I don't like talking on the subject, but it's difficult to resist someone so sympathetic as you. We're all children really and like to go and sob in mummy's arms."

His companion was not too pleased at the comparison.

"I'm not as old as all that."

"You old? Whoever suggested it? Oh—mummy's arms, you mean. Just a simile, you know."

"Well, try a better one next time."

"I'm dreadfully sorry. You're so terribly attractive that I should simply adore being in your arms."

"Sobbing?"

"Anything at all. But don't let's talk of my life any more. What about you?"

And Ronald would leave the sad story of his noble past. In point of fact there was no basis for the story at all. Had Ronald fallen in love with the wife of his best friend, and had the lady responded, there is little doubt but that they would have gone off together. Fortunately for all concerned, it never happened. But on occasions it made a good excuse for his never having married.

Jane Doughty, the youngest daughter of his next-door neighbors, had been fond of Ronald as a child and he of her. Her parents encouraged the friendship. As she grew older the tie between her and Ronald became stronger and stronger, and by the time she was ten he was an extra father. Colonel and Mrs. Doughty were delighted. They had a wide circle of friends and enjoyed a busy social life. Their two elder daughters were grown up, and Jane might have been a slight problem but for Ronald. But he was nearly always ready to come in and look after Jane. He had no parents, no wife, no children. Jane helped to fill the gap. He had strong paternal instincts and it was a great joy to him to know that Jane was next door. It appeared a healthy, happy friendship and no one realized the possible dangers involved.

At the age of twelve Jane broke into verse. She rushed around to No. 18 with her first effort.

"Look at this, Ronnieboy," she said.

When she had first started to speak she had said something which sounded like "Ronnieboy," a name which no one, not even his mother, had called him. But it stuck. And to Jane he was always Ronnieboy.

"Listen," she said, and began to recite proudly:

> There was a little thing
> And it had a piece of string
> And it sat on the edge of the basin.

"You must say 'basin' rather strongly," she interposed, "something like *ba*-sin. You'll see why in a moment. I'll start again.

> "There was a little thing
> And it had a piece of string
> And it sat on the edge of the *ba*-sin
> And it wished for a wish
> And it fished for a fish
> And then it put its little face in.

"You must say the last line rather quickly. And now you see why I said *ba*-sin? To go with 'face in.' D'you like it, Ronnieboy?"

"Jolly good," said Ronald. "Let's see if I can remember it. 'There was a little thing, And—and . . .' "

" 'It had a piece of string,' " prompted Jane.

" 'And it sat on the edge of the *ba*-sin.' "

"You needn't overdo it," said Jane.

"Sorry," said Ronald. " 'And it sat on the edge of the *ba*-sin.' Is that better?"

"Much."

" 'And it fished for a fish.' "

"No, the other way round. 'Wish' comes first."

" 'And it wished for a wish, and it fished for a fish . . .' " Here Ronald paused for so long that Jane said:

"Surely you've not forgotten the best line?"

"No," said Ronald, "but I think it wants a pause after 'fish,' and that makes hurrying the last line more effective. Like this:

> "And it wished for a wish
> And it fished for a fish . . .
> And-then-it-put-its-little-face-in.

"How's that?"

"Oh, that's lovely, Ronnieboy," said Jane, and clapped her hands.

And he did it again. And again. And just once more. And once for luck. And just once, all for me. And one for you. And now a lovely one all for us.

Often on a Sunday, when Colonel Doughty was playing golf and Mrs. Doughty too busy in the house, Ronald would take Jane to church. She loved going anywhere with him, but particularly to church. Sometimes he read the Lessons and Jane would sit entranced. He had quite a good voice and was inclined to dramatize, even to overdramatize, what he read.

> "Dost thou appeal to Caesar?
> Unto Caesar thou shalt go,"

he once read, with considerable emphasis and some venom in the last line. Jane very nearly clapped.

"I'm glad everyone doesn't read like you," she said afterward.

"Don't you like the way I read?"

"I love it. You know I do. That's why I should hate anyone else to do it like you. It wouldn't be right. Oh, I do love you, Ronnieboy. So much, so very much. So everything. Please don't die. That would be terrible. There was a girl at school lost both parents. I don't know what I'd do if I lost you. You'll never leave me, will you? Promise. Never, never, never. Never-never-never," she rattled off.

" 'And-then-it-put-its-little-face-in,' " Ronald rattled off in reply.

"You don't laugh at me, Ronnieboy, do you?"

"Of course I do, sometimes, like you laugh at me."

"No, seriously I mean. At my loving you so much."

"Of course not," said Ronald. "You're very precious to me."

" 'Precious,' what a lovely word. Diamonds and rubies and emeralds—and me. Precious me. Say I'm precious."

"You're very precious."

"More precious than diamonds?"

"Far above rubies."

"Where does that come from?"

"You tell me."

"The Bible?"

"Yes. Now tell me what is far above rubies."

"I am."

"Of course. What else?"

"It's your turn, Ronnieboy. I've done one."

"Well, wisdom for one thing. But there's another."

"What is it?"

"A virtuous woman."

"Am I a virtuous woman?"

"You will be."

"Do virtuous women have fun? I don't want to be like the Albert Memorial, all stuck up and nowhere to go."

"Oh, yes," said Ronald, "virtuous women have a fine time. It's the other sort I'm sorry for."

"What do unvirtuous women do, then?"

"Oh, all sorts of things."

"When *I* say 'all sorts of things,' Ronnieboy, you say that might mean anything."

"When do you say 'all sorts of things'?"

"When I come back from a holiday or something, and you ask me what I've done and I say 'All sorts of things.' Then you want to know what sort of things. Now *I* do."

"I'll tell you when you're older."

"Oh, no, not you too, Ronnieboy. That's what Mummy says. Don't you know that today people tell children everything?"

"Do they now?"

"You know they do. I know all about being born and all that. So what do unvirtuous women do?"

"Well, they're good for nothing, or very little."

"What does that mean?"

"Well, they're layabouts."

"But that's a lovely word. I love laying about—or is it lying about? Am I a layabout?"

"Certainly not. A layabout is a lazy, worthless person, who never does anything himself or herself and just gets what he or she can from other people."

"What a shame. It sounds so friendly—a layabout. What else do unvirtuous women do, apart from laying about?"

"Well, some of them get married and go about with other men just as though they weren't married at all."

"How dreadful. 'And forsaking all others, keep thee only unto him so long as ye both shall live.' That's what you mean, isn't it?"

"D'you know the marriage service by heart?"

"Not all of it, but I love it so. I, Jane, take you, Ronnieboy, to be my wedded husband, to have and to hold and something and to cherish—that's another lovely word—to cherish and to be with always and always, in sickness and in health, for richer, for poorer, and something till death us do part. Oh, please, please don't let death us part."

"Well, I hope it won't for a long time," said Ronald, "and that, when it does, you'll have a husband to comfort you."

"But you're my husband."

"I'm much too old to be anyone's husband. I should have married years ago if I was going to marry at all."

Some people in Eleanor Gardens did occasionally comment on the close relationship between Jane and Ronald. But nobody did anything about it, until it was too late. It began when Jane was sixteen, and Ronald then started to have misgivings. But he was far too comfortable and easygoing to do anything about it at first. Moreover, not only had Jane become very useful to him, starting to look after him, to do things for him as a wife almost or a fond mistress, but he loved her deeply. Purely paternally. She had grown up almost as a daughter to him and she filled a very real need in his heart. Someone to be desperately fond of. But not sexually in the least. That would have seemed incestuous to him.

But by the time she was seventeen there was no doubt what Jane wanted. And on the day before Ronald visited Highcastle and Newbury she had said so outright. Although he had realized what was happening, he had shut his mind to it. And when Jane said, "If you won't marry me, please, please sleep with me, Ronnieboy. At least I want you to be the first," he was horrified. In one second his relationship with Jane suddenly became a nightmare to him. The idea of his being anything to her but a father, godfather or uncle was as repulsive as the idea of a homosexual act is to a heterosexual. It was repugnant and indecent. A feeling of loathing came over him. He simply couldn't stand it. The fact that it was his fault for allowing such a close relationship to begin and to be fully maintained made no difference. He realized all of a sudden that he would simply not be able to bear the look of longing desire in Jane's eyes.

He had only one thought. He must get out. He would have to stay in London, as all his friends and interests were there. But away from Jane. He did spare a moment or two to be sorry for the girl, but he was far too concerned with his own horror to think much about her. As a baby he had once been taken from his high chair to be shown to visitors when his face was sticky. As a result he always had an unpleasant feeling if his hands or face was sticky. He always washed them at once if possible. But that was a trifle. Now, in a far, far stronger way he felt that, as long as he was anywhere near Jane, he would have a feeling of uncleanness. He must wash it out of his system, and the only way he could ever do that would be by permanent and complete separation, and as soon as possible. But there mustn't be any scandal, or people in their kindly way might assume all sorts of things. He would simply say that he had had a good offer for his house and couldn't afford to refuse it.

The day after he had put his house in agents' hands, the telephone rang. It was Mr. Highcastle.

"As you're in a hurry to sell," he said, "I thought it would be a good idea to advertise—from a box number, of course, so that no one will know it's you. I thought of something like this: 'Very desirable—' "

"Not that word," interrupted Ronald. "Call it splendid or beautiful, or tell any other lie, but don't call it desirable. I can't stand the word." He said it so fiercely that Mr. Highcastle said almost complainingly:

"I'm sorry, sir. It's a very usual word, if I may say so. It doesn't really mean anything."

"Then why use it? No one takes any notice of your advertisements, anyway. Why not just call it a house? After all, that's what it is. It isn't beautiful, elegant or splendid. Least of all is it desirable."

"Surely, sir," said the agent, "if someone wants it, it is desirable?"

5

Order to View

A PERSON WHO NORMALLY TELLS THE TRUTH has a clear conscience to protect, or at least to comfort him, when he is wrongly suspected of telling a lie. But a man like Ronald, who is perfectly prepared to lie when he thinks it necessary, has nothing to fall back on when he tells the truth and is disbelieved. It is very galling for him, as Ronald found when showing his house to Mr. and Mrs. Abbot. They were the first prospective buyers of No. 18 and they came from Manchester.

"This is the drawing room," said Ronald.

"You mean the lounge," said Mr. Abbot.

"If you buy it, you can call it what you like," replied Ronald.

"I can do that, whether I buy it or not," said Mr. Abbot. "It's a free country."

"Really, dear," protested Mrs. Abbot.

"Mr. Holbrook wants to sell his house," said Mr. Abbot, "and, as long as he thinks there's a chance of my buying it, he isn't going to quarrel over what I call it. Or him," he added. "It's Colonel Holbrook, as a matter of fact, isn't it?"

"Oh, that's quite all right," said Ronald.

"See what I mean, dear?" said Mr. Abbot.

They walked around the room.

"Can I look at the back of that picture?" asked Mr. Abbot.

"Oh, it's not an original," said Ronald.

"It'd be all the same to me if it were," said Mr. Abbot. "What's wrong with a photograph, anyway? If you like the picture, one's as good as the other if you ask me. And, if you don't, the same. Can I look?"

"Certainly," said Ronald, "but you won't find anything."

"I hope not," said Mr. Abbot. "I'm looking for damp spots. Some people—" he added, "I'm not suggesting you—but some people put up pictures like this to hide the damp spots."

"I assure you—" began Ronald, and stopped, horrified.

Behind the picture was a large patch of dried damp.

"I had no idea," protested Ronald.

"Lucky I had," said Mr. Abbot, and winked.

"I don't know what it can be," said Ronald.

"We'll find out and let you know," said Mr. Abbot. "That's if you'll pay the surveyor's fee. But we won't bother about a surveyor if there are too many of these. Does the central heating work?"

"Certainly."

"This radiator's cold."

"We don't need it on a day like this."

"Is it turned off at the main?"

"No."

"Then may I turn this on, just to be sure?"

"Of course, if you want to."

Mr. Abbot turned on the radiator.

"Bit stiff, isn't it?" he said. "Anyway, we'll have a look at it on the way out."

"I was told to ask if you'd want any of the fittings, carpets and curtains," said Ronald.

"Hold hard," said Mr. Abbot. "We haven't even said we liked the house yet, let alone agreed to buy it. You'll take an offer, I imagine?"

"I leave that sort of thing to the agent," said Ronald.

"More's the pity," said Mr. Abbot. "Couple of hundred down

the drain for nothing. Now, if we could say we'd already had the house from a friend of yours but didn't remember the address till we got here, we could cut out the agent and share the commission between us. Not that I'd do anything that wasn't aboveboard. I'm sure you wouldn't want to, either."

"You mean," said Ronald, "that, if a friend of mine had already given you the name of the house, I shouldn't have to pay commission to the agents?"

"That's right," said Mr. Abbot. "They're shocking parasites, anyway, agents. Like most middlemen. Some of them are downright dishonest—take commissions from both sides and all that sort of thing."

"How d'you mean?"

"Don't you know that? You're ripe for plucking, I must say. Well, you want to sell a house for seven thousand pounds. I want to buy it for six thousand. I say to the agent, 'If you can get this for me for six thousand I'll give you one hundred pounds.' So the agent persuades you to sell at the lower figure. He only loses fifteen pounds on his commission from you and he gets one hundred pounds from me. I gain and he gains. You're the one who loses."

"I never thought of that," said Ronald.

"Come to think of it, it might be happening in this case, for all you know. Let's turn the tables on him. Then *he'd* be the odd man out. What was the name of that friend of yours who told me about it? Who d'you know in Manchester?"

"Manchester? Manchester . . . ?" said Ronald. "I know a parson there."

"Don't think a parson would do. They might ask him. But let's see the house a bit first. I'm not all that keen on it. Are you, dear?"

"It has a lovely kitchen," said Mrs. Abbot.

"Now, we're not eating in the kitchen," said Mr. Abbot. "We finished with that twenty years ago."

"I often eat in the kitchen, as a matter of fact," said Ronald. "And it's handy when Jane makes me an omelet."

"Your wife, I suppose?"

"No, as a matter of fact, it's the girl next door."

Ronald colored as he said this. Mr. Abbot winked.

"Ah!" he said. "The girl next door. Is she thrown in with the fixtures and fittings?"

"Dear!" protested Mrs. Abbot.

"Mr.—Colonel Holbrook won't mind my bit of fun, so long as we might be buyers, will you?" asked Mr. Abbot.

"I'd prefer just to discuss the house," said Ronald, who had mentioned Jane quite automatically and was much regretting it.

"It's like that, is it?" said Mr. Abbot. "I won't say another word," and he made a knowing gesture with his finger down the side of his nose. "Now let's see upstairs, please," he went on. "The bedroom floor," he added.

They went upstairs.

"Couldn't very well have pictures on the ceiling," said Mr. Abbot, pointing to a patch of damp.

"We had a loose slate. It's been repaired," said Ronald.

"How long ago?"

"About six months."

"Only one slate?"

"I think so."

"Got the bill?"

"No, I paid by check."

"You could still have a receipt, if you asked for one."

"I didn't."

"I always do. Now that banks only show numbers, it's the best way. Counterfoil could be wrong. Anyway, you haven't had the ceiling redone. That because you're waiting to see if some more comes through first?"

"Really, sir," began Ronald.

"Only my little joke," said Mr. Abbot. "Ask the wife. She'll tell you. I'm full of fun. Too much, they said at school. But it's good in business. Make the other fellow laugh and he'll forget what he was worrying about. Which reminds me. Haven't made you laugh much. P'raps you don't, though."

"This is the spare bedroom," said Ronald. "You could make a study of it, if you wanted to."

"Mind if I look at the back of the pictures?"

"There *is* a little damp in this room," said Ronald quickly.

"Glad you've remembered," said Mr. Abbot. "Well, where is

it?" he said. He turned back each of the pictures with no result.

"It's behind that desk, as a matter of fact," said Ronald.

"Goodness gracious," said Mr. Abbot. "I must be slipping. That's bigger than all the pictures put together, and I nearly missed it. That only goes to show, doesn't it? And what's the cause of this?"

"The lavatory overflowed, Ball cock broke, or something."

"Ah, the lavatory. The one downstairs could do with a bit of spit and polish. This one the same?"

"I was told that you'd probably want to redecorate and that it would be best to let you choose your own scheme."

"You were told? By the agent, I suppose."

"Yes, as a matter of fact."

"Well, that's something for your fifty percent."

Ronald looked horrified.

"Fifty percent!" he said. "But I thought—"

"More fun," said Mr. Abbot. "Let's have a look at this lavatory. Humph," he said, when he looked inside. "What's the speed of the flush? May I try it?"

"Please do," said Ronald.

Mr. Abbot pulled the chain. It came down easily, too easily. There was a slight gurgle, but no flush.

"It usually works," said Ronald.

"Once a month?" queried Mr. Abbot. "Could be awkward if one had a party."

"Let me try it," said Ronald, and he gave the chain several ineffective pulls.

"I'll have it seen to," he said eventually.

"I should," said Mr. Abbot. "Now let me show you something. Look at my shoes, please, dear," he said to his wife. He held up first one foot and then the other for his wife to inspect the soles.

"All right?" he asked.

"Yes, dear."

"Right," said Mr. Abbot.

He then got up and stood on the seat and pressed the lever hard down. Immediately the apparatus flushed. Mr. Abbot got down, dusted his hands against each other.

"Simple," he said. "My name's in the phone book. Call me any time you want me."

"I didn't think there was anything really wrong," said Ronald gratefully.

"Just wants a complete new outfit," said Mr. Abbot.

"But it works," protested Ronald.

"So do a lot of *people*, but not hard enough. They take off too much time. Fine thing if I had to go in after every guest and do that. Now let's see, how many bedrooms have you got?"

"Four."

"The agent said 'possibly five.' Where's the fifth? The coal cellar?"

"It's rather a small room," said Ronald apologetically. "Up those few steps. Oh—mind your head," he added quickly, but too late. "I'm terribly sorry," he said.

Mr. Abbot grimaced in pain, and said nothing for a moment.

"If I have headaches after this, you'll have to pay," he said eventually. "How could I tell the top of the door was so low?"

"Well, you *could* actually see," said Ronald.

"D'you think I did it on purpose?" asked Mr. Abbot, and felt his head gently. "I shall have a lump on there like a walnut."

"It is rather deceptive," admitted Ronald.

"All I can say is I hope you're insured against such risks," said Mr. Abbot. "Well, how big d'you call this?" he asked as he opened the door. "Five by five?"

"It's seven by six, as a matter of fact," said Ronald.

"That's how my head feels," said Mr. Abbot. "Come on, dear, I've had enough."

"Then perhaps you'll let me know—or the agent," asked Ronald, as they reached the front door.

"I'm letting you know now," said Mr. Abbot. "Good morning."

6

Another Order to View

MR. AND MRS. CRANE were the next to view Ronald's house. Mr.
Highcastle brought them. After his experience of the Abbots,
Ronald felt that it would be far better if the agent could do all
the explaining.

"Well, I'll come when I can," said Mr. Highcastle, "but I shan't
be able to manage it each time."

"Perhaps the next people will take it," said Ronald.

"If you lowered the price, they might," said Mr. Highcastle.

The Cranes were very different from the Abbots.

"This is the lounge," said Mr. Highcastle. "Charming room,
don't you think?"

"Very," said Mrs. Crane.

"Quite," said her husband.

"You could easily have a dance in here," went on Mr. Highcastle.

"Oh, yes," said Mrs. Crane.

"I see," said her husband.

"The dining room's opposite," said Mr. Highcastle. "Plenty of
room there too."

As they passed across the hall to go into the dining room, the front door opened and Jane walked in. Ronald had to think quickly.

"Hullo," said Jane.

"This is Jane Doughty from next door," said Ronald. "Mr. and Mrs. Crane and Mr. Castle."

It was comparatively easy to convey Highcastle to Mr. Castle and Castle to Jane.

"Excuse me a moment," Ronald said. "I want to speak to Jane for a minute."

He took her outside the house.

"These are some people I haven't seen for years," he said. "They want to come and live in the neighborhood. I met them some years ago and they found my name in the phone book. So they asked if they could come and look at the inside of my house."

"Do we want them here, Ronnieboy?"

"I think they'd fit in very well."

"Right," said Jane. "I'll come and say how wonderful it is."

"Oh, I shouldn't bother," said Ronald. "We shan't be long."

"But I'd like to," said Jane. "I haven't seen you for twelve whole hours. Come along."

She seized his arm and took him into the house enthusiastically.

"This place is absolutely super," she announced to the Cranes and Mr. Highcastle. "You should certainly come and live here."

"I see," said Mr. Crane.

"It's beautifully quiet," said Jane.

"I rather like a certain amount of bustle," said Mrs. Crane. "Quite frankly, I don't like things too quiet."

"Then you don't like the country?"

"Not like the country? Of course I do. Far noisier than most parts of town. The dawn chorus makes much more noise than the milkman, and starts earlier too. In the summer, anyway. And what with cows and sheep, I'm well away."

"The milkmen are pretty good around here," said Jane. "And they drop a bottle every now and then. One of them's quite a friend of mine. I'll ask him to stir up things a bit, if you come."

"That's most kind," said Mrs. Crane.

"And the dustmen come early sometimes," went on Jane. "You'll get plenty of bustle from them."

"Only once a week," put in Ronald. He was not sure that the shouts and clatter of the dustmen would necessarily appeal to someone who liked animal noises.

While they were going around the house, Ronald managed to take Mr. Highcastle on one side.

"For heaven's sake don't let her know what you're here for. She's the reason I want things kept quiet."

"I quite understand," said Mr. Highcastle, in a tone which indicated that he did not.

The Cranes, like most people who inspect houses, said very little beyond "I see" or "Oh, yes" when any particular part or aspect of the house was pointed out to them. Certainly they said nothing which was not as consistent with their wanting to live in the neighborhood as with their wanting to buy this particular house. Ronald realized, however, that the most delicate part of the interview would be when they were going. He tried unsuccessfully to get rid of Jane before they left. So he made up his mind what to do. When they had completed their inspection, he rather hustled the three of them to the front door, shook them all warmly by the hand and said:

"Well, good-bye, old man. So very nice to have seen you. Hope you decide to come and live here," and without waiting for a reply, shut the door almost in their faces so as to avoid giving them a chance to say anything.

"Why were you so rude to them, Ronnieboy?" asked Jane. "It's not like you at all."

"Was I?" said Ronald. "I didn't mean to be. I'll go and apologize." And, without giving Jane a chance to follow, he opened the front door and went out and caught up with his three visitors as they were getting into a car.

"So sorry about that," he said quickly, "but as I explained to Mr. Highcastle, I don't want anyone to know I'm leaving. So sorry. Good-bye."

He went back to the house. Jane was already outside the front door. She took his arm and brought him inside.

"This is all rather mysterious," she said. "What are you up to?"

"Up to? Up to?" repeated Ronald, sounding as surprised as he could. "What on earth d'you mean?"

"You're not thinking of doing a bolt, Ronnieboy?"

"Why should I?"

"I can't think of a reason," said Jane, "and I don't want to. But it all seemed very odd. Just as though one of them was an agent and the other two people he was showing over the house."

"Don't be absurd," said Ronald. "I've been here for twenty years. What's the point in leaving now?"

"Promise you won't leave, except with me."

"I promise," said Ronald without the slightest hesitation.

"Good," said Jane. "Now make love to me."

"No," said Ronald firmly.

"Why not?" asked Jane. "You love me and I love you, and I'm over age. Why not?"

"It would be wrong."

"Old enough to be my father, and all that stuff?"

"Not just that, though that's something. But it's wrong and you must know it."

"Get back to the Ark," said Jane. "Everyone does it."

"Everyone does *not* do it," said Ronald.

"Well, more fool they," said Jane. "What's wrong with it? You're not married, nor am I, and it's a pleasant thing to do."

"How d'you know?"

"I just know it would be. And I want you to be the first."

"Well, I'm not going to be. Find someone nearer your own age. No, I didn't mean that," he added hastily.

"I will, if you're not careful," said Jane. "And anyway, you said it. That means it's not wrong in itself. I know St. Paul was against it. But he was against a lot of things. He was against Christ once. But he changed his mind. If he can change his mind on a big subject like that, surely you can change yours on a little one like making love to me. Don't you want to?"

"No," said Ronald. "I've told you."

"Aren't I pretty enough?"

"You're very pretty."

"Too thin? Too fat?"

"You've a lovely figure."

"Then what are you waiting for? Here I am. All for you."

"I'm very fond of you, Jane," said Ronald, "but not that way."

"You could try."

"No."

"Why not? If you wanted to, would you? Is it really because you think it's wrong, or because you don't want to?"

"Both."

"Both? I hate you. You're beastly. You might at least pretend you wanted me. I believe you do really. You're just doing the right thing and trying to make it easy for me."

"All right, we'll say it's that."

"Oh, darling," said Jane, and kissed him. "It's lovely to know you really want me. That's something. Look at me, Ronnieboy. Am I very desirable?"

"Now, be a good girl, Jane, and go back home."

"Everyone's out. It's a wonderful chance. I'd do anything you wanted."

Ronald felt physically sick, but couldn't bring himself to say so.

"Go home, please, Jane. I've got a lot to do."

"What sort of things?"

"All sorts."

"Such as what?"

"Some letters to write."

"They'll keep."

"They really won't."

"Who are they to?"

"I'm not going to tell you."

"I don't believe there are any. Tell me one of them."

Ronald thought quickly.

"I've got a query about my income-tax accounts."

"That can't be urgent."

"It is. I ought to have answered it ages ago."

"Then a few more hours won't hurt. Let me sit on your knee."

"Not now."

"I always used to."

"You were younger."

"You mean you can't stand it if I'm close to you. You're frightened of giving way. Is that it?"

"Call it that."

"Oh, how lovely. If my body was next to yours, you'd feel you'd have to make love to me. Suppose I undressed—would that do the same?"

"Definitely not."

Ronald spoke almost harshly.

"Why so definite? You've seen me naked lots of times. The body's the same. Just a bit older. That's all."

"Fifteen years older," said Ronald.

"It's interesting now," said Jane. "A baby's body's only interesting to its parents. I'm a woman now, and I'm interesting to men. And you're a man. And you're my man. Oh, Ronnieboy—Ronnieboy, please always be my man."

"Go home," said Ronald.

Jane frowned.

"All right," she said. "I'll go now. But I'll make you one day. I'll make you. I really will."

7

The Ultimatum

THE SAME AFTERNOON Ronald went again to Highcastle and Newbury. Mr. Highcastle was out and Ronald was interviewed by a
young man with a tired voice.

"You haven't sent me any houses," Ronald began.

"To view?" asked the young man.

"To buy," said Ronald. "As quickly as possible."

"You want to buy a house?"

"At once."

"It says here you want to sell. Eleanor Gardens."

"I do."

"Not buy, sell."

"I want to buy another house."

"In Eleanor Gardens?"

"As far away from Eleanor Gardens as possible."

The young man thought for a few moments.

"The other side of London, you mean?"

"That will do very well."

"How about Putney?"

"Putney?"

"That's southwest. Eleanor Gardens is north."

"Have you got some houses in Putney?"

"We can get them."

The young man picked up a telephone and dialed a number.

"Swears and Killick? We've got a client who wants a house in Putney at once. Just a moment."

He reached for a piece of paper.

"Twelve Claremont Road," he repeated, "two reception, four bed, partial central heating, garden, garage. Ninety-five hundred pounds. How's that, sir?" he asked Ronald. "I expect they'll knock a bit off the price."

"I'll go and see it at once," said Ronald.

An hour later Ronald rang the bell of 12 Claremont Road. It was opened by a woman.

"D'you mind if I ask you a question before we go around the house?" she asked.

"Not at all."

"Are you a serious buyer at ninety-five hundred? Please forgive me for asking, but I've shown so many people around, and I'm sick to death of it. Some of them can't get a mortgage, most of them want to knock something off the price, and I can't think why some of the people come at all."

"Ninety-five hundred is rather a lot," said Ronald.

"It may or may not be a lot, but that's the price, I'm afraid. Did they tell you I'd take less?"

"It was suggested."

"Well, it shouldn't have been. I won't even throw in the curtains and carpets. You can buy them, of course, at a fair price, but I'm not selling at less than ninety-five hundred."

"I see," said Ronald. "I wonder if I might use the telephone?" he added after a pause.

"They do that too," said the woman. "There's one at the corner. It's only about three hundred yards down the road."

"It looks like rain," said Ronald, putting on some of his charm. I wonder if—" but this was not one of Ronald's good days.

"A little rain doesn't do anyone any harm," said the woman.

"You're very kind," said Ronald with his most charming smile, so charming that even the woman began to think she had been a little hasty. But by the time she was thinking of inviting him in, he was too far down the street.

Ronald called Highcastle and Newbury and was glad to find Mr. Highcastle had returned. He explained what had happened.

"I'm glad you telephoned," said Mr. Highcastle. "There's a pleasant little house quite close. Seven Derbyshire Avenue. Anyone will tell you where it is. Just about your size and the price should be right."

Ronald thanked Mr. Highcastle and began to search for Derbyshire Avenue. He had no success.

"Derbyshire Road?" the third person queried.

"No, Avenue."

"I don't know of an avenue. Are you sure there's no mistake?"

"Well, I'll try the road. Thank you very much."

"Well, that's very simple. You can't miss it. Go straight down here. Take the first small turning on the left. Not the little alleyway. That's a dead end. You'll find a public house at the corner. Don't go down that road, but carry on for about three or four hundred yards. I'll tell you how many turnings it is. Two—no, three—no, bless me, four. Would you believe it, I've lived here twenty-five years and I can't be sure of the number of turnings. Let me think. There's Glossop Lane, Barleycroft Road, no, confound it, it's Beechcroft Road, Barleycroft is the other side of the main road, the Upper Richmond Road, I mean, not the High Street. Now, where was I? Oh, yes: two turnings after Beechcroft Road you'll see a mailbox—well, you won't see it at first because it's not a standing one but let into the wall of a house and it faces the other way, stupid of me, really, I'm always doing that, telling people there's a mailbox and then of course they can't see it. And what makes it worse is that, if you look down that turning—what's it called? Hollybourne Street, of course—if you look down Hollybourne Street, about two hundred yards down the road there's a standing mailbox, so people get confused and walk down to it, and by that time they're really lost. It isn't Hollybourne Street. That's by the cinema. It's Holbein Street. One oughtn't to mix them up really. There wasn't a painter called Hollybourne."

"Oh, yes there was," said Ronald. "Mid-eighteenth century.

Mostly did portraits, but a few landscapes. Thank you so much. Good morning."

Ronald asked a few more times and eventually found Derbyshire Road. And there in the middle of it was a for-sale sign and when he got to the house it was No. 7. He rang the bell and waited. The door was opened by a man.

"I wonder—" began Ronald.

"Sold last week, I'm afraid," said the man. "So sorry. I'm afraid it's rather an awkward place to find."

Ronald went unhappily home. Jane was waiting for him.

"Where have you been?"

"Just for a stroll."

"Why didn't you take me?"

"I'd a problem to think out."

"Couldn't I have helped? Just by listening, I mean."

The bell rang and Jane went to answer it. The callers were strangers. A man and a woman.

"We have an order to view," said the man, and flourished a piece of paper.

"An order to view?" said Jane. "Oh, I see. Ronnieboy," she called, "someone's come about the house. About the house," she added meaningly.

"I'll explain," said Ronald softly to her, as he came to the door.

"You'd better," said Jane.

"From Highcastle and Newbury?" asked Ronald.

"Yes," said the man. "May we have a look around?"

"Of course," said Ronald.

The viewers were of the silent sort and contented themselves with "Ohs" and "Ahs" and very occasional adjectives: "charming," "nice and large," "rather small," and so on.

Eventually the woman said:

"It seems delightfully quiet here."

"That's one of the things we must have," said the man.

"Apart from airplanes," began Jane.

"They're less frequent than they were," put in Ronald.

"D'you like singing?" asked Jane.

"Singing? Why?" asked the man.

"My mother sings," said Jane. "We live next door, you know. She's awfully good."

"Does she practice much?"

"Good gracious, yes," said Jane. "You'll enjoy it. She's only an amateur, but she sings a lot in comic opera and that sort of thing. Gilbert and Sullivan and all that. She played the fairy queen in *Iolanthe*. And she's rehearsing for Katisha in *The Mikado* at the moment. If you wait a bit, you might hear her. The walls aren't all that thick. My father *doesn't* sing. He plays the clarinet *and* the oboe."

"We shall be able to hear him too, I suppose," said the man grimly.

"Oh, yes, indeed," said Jane. "The present occupier loves it."

"It's only a joke," said Ronald.

Jane looked at him.

"Ronnieboy," she said, "how *can* you? You wouldn't want the lady and gentleman to buy the place under false pretenses."

"Jane, go home," said Ronald quite sharply.

"Very well," said Jane. "I know when I'm not wanted."

She left hurriedly and Ronald began to explain that neither of Jane's parents had any connection whatever with music.

"As I said, it's her idea of a joke."

A moment later the most horrible noise came from next door. It was Jane trying to imitate a high soprano and several cats.

"That's only Jane," said Ronald.

"I'm afraid," said the man, "that high-spirited young ladies like that are not for us as neighbors. I'm so sorry."

"She's never done it before," said Ronald.

"That doesn't mean to say she won't do it again," said the woman. "So very sorry to have troubled you."

Jane, looking out of a window, saw them go, and within seconds came back to Ronald.

"What *is* this?" she asked. "That's what those other people were here for, wasn't it?"

"I've got to get away from you," said Ronald. "It's not good for you and it's not fair to you."

"What are you talking about? You love me, don't you?"

"Not the way you want," said Ronald, "and it just won't do."

"It's just going to do," said Jane. "If you think I'm going to let you run out on me, you've made a big mistake. It's sneak out, more like. Pretending those other people were old friends. Oh, Ronnieboy, how could you? How could you lie to me? I've always trusted you so absolutely. And then you tell the most beastly lot of lies. Oh, Ronnieboy—Ronnieboy." And she burst into tears.

Ronald tried to comfort her.

"Now you must be sensible. You're grown up now."

"I know," she sobbed, "that's what I've been telling you. I want you to treat me as a woman."

Ronald sighed.

"I think I'll have to speak to your parents," he said.

"Say what to them?"

"Tell them how unhappy you are."

"You mean you'll tell them I want to go to bed with you. If you do, Ronnieboy, if you do, I'll tell them I have."

"In that case they'll certainly be glad I'm leaving."

"You might go out feet first," said Jane. "Certainly you'd be on a stretcher. Daddy's not normally a violent man, but if he thought you'd seduced me he'd pretty well kill you. There'd only be your word against mine."

"You're a very wicked little girl," said Ronald.

"I'm not really," said Jane, "but I must fight for you. Life will be nothing for me if I lose you. And I'll stop at nothing to keep you. Nothing. I'm not wicked, you know I'm not. But you're my whole life and I've got to keep you."

"I don't know what to do with you," said Ronald.

"I could tell you," said Jane.

"Don't, please, Jane," said Ronald. "It's disgusting."

"All right, Ronnieboy, I won't—so long as you don't go away. So long as I can keep you, I'll try to be good. Not be too animal, I mean. But I do feel terribly animal, Ronnieboy. Couldn't you be animal too—just once?"

"You said you wouldn't," said Ronald.

"But you haven't promised to stay."

"All right, I promise."

"Then ring up the agents and say you don't want to sell the house."

"I can't."

"But why not? You've promised to stay. What's the point of letting people come to see the house if you're not going to sell it?"

"I just don't know what to do."

"But you've promised to stay. If you don't keep your word, I needn't keep mine. And I certainly don't want to keep it. You aren't going away, are you?"

"I must."

"But you promised only a moment ago."

"I would stay if I could, but it'll be impossible."

"Well, if you go, I'll go with you."

"You couldn't do that."

"Who's to stop me?"

"Your parents."

"They couldn't lock me in all the time. Anyway, they wouldn't."

"If I tried to take you away from them they could get a court order to stop me."

"How lovely that sounds. If you tried to take me away . . . I wish you would."

"The court could stop us both. They could order me not to take you away, and you not to come with me. And they could send us to prison if we disobeyed."

"I wouldn't mind going to prison for you."

"Well, I should very much mind going to prison for you, or any-one else. But I shouldn't be sent to prison, as I shouldn't have taken you away."

"Then they couldn't send me to prison, either."

"Oh, yes, they could. If you were ordered not to come with me and you broke the order, you could be sent to prison."

"But who's going to order me?"

"The court."

"But somebody would have to ask the court first. Daddy and Mummy wouldn't have me sent to prison."

"They might prefer you there than in my bed."

"Oh, Ronnieboy, would you really take me there?"

"Certainly not. On no account. But your parents might think that would happen."

"Well, I'll risk it. If you go, I go."

"Where will you live?"

"With you."

"But I wouldn't have that."

"How could you stop it? Would you have me beating at the door to get in?"

"The police would take you away."

"But you wouldn't let them, Ronnieboy. You wouldn't do that."

"I might have to."

Jane kept silent for a short time.

"I can see that I've got to speak to you seriously," she said. "You don't seem to believe that I mean what I say. You said I was wicked, a little time back. Well, I'm not really, but I *could* be over you. And I could be a good deal wickeder than that."

"What d'you mean?"

"Only that I'll stop at nothing to keep you."

"You've said that several times."

"But you don't seem to realize that it's true. I'll make life hell for you, if you don't stay. What a terrible thing to say when I love you so much. But I know I mean it. You'll have to surrender, Ronnieboy. I've got all the cards."

"What are you threatening?"

"Nothing—if you stay."

"Suppose I speak to your parents?"

"You said that before, and I told you what I'd say."

"You could be proved wrong. I'd ask your parents to have you medically examined."

"Oh, Ronnieboy, how stupid can you be? D'you think I hadn't thought of that? You don't imagine I haven't met a few would-be boyfriends? I'd soon have the proof, all right."

"You're just being indecent."

"I'll be worse before I'm finished. If you don't promise to stay— and keep your word—I'll have a baby and say it's yours. How will you get over that? You don't imagine the real father will want to come along, and you won't know who he is, anyway. It'll just be word against word. And we've had lots of opportunities. We could be in bed together now, for all anyone knew. I wish we were. Oh, Ronnieboy, if only we were. I'd make it up to you. There's nothing I wouldn't do for you."

"Nothing you wouldn't do for me," said Ronald. "Apparently there isn't. I'd no idea what a bitch you were. I wouldn't have thought it possible."

"Go on, call me names, Ronnieboy, I love it. Put some adjectives to them. I love you calling me a bitch. I *am* one. Go on, say it again. I love it. Hit me. With your hand or just with words. I don't mind which. Only do things to me, Ronnieboy, do things to me."

8

Mr. Plumb

THE NEXT DAY RONALD MADE AN APPOINTMENT to see a solicitor, Mr. Plumb, of Slograve, Plumb and Co. Mr. Plumb was a mournful-looking man, and his manner of speech was in keeping with his appearance.

"Good morning," he said to Ronald on the day of the appointment. "I don't think I've had the pleasure."

"Fortunately I haven't needed a solicitor for some time. And my last one's dead."

"I'm so sorry," said Mr. Plumb.

"It was fifteen years ago."

"Life's but a walking shadow," said Mr. Plumb. "May I ask who introduced you?"

"No one," said Ronald. "I picked you out with a pin, I'm afraid. I liked the name."

"Strange," said Mr. Plumb. "I've never liked my name, Joseph Plumb. It's easy to remember, I suppose, and unpretentious, but I've never liked it. Perhaps it's because boys used to laugh at it at school. I still remember being asked my name and the titter which followed my answer. Once the master intervened. 'What's funny

43

about Joseph Plumb?' he said. 'It's the way he said it, sir,' said one of the boys, and tried to imitate me. 'The way he said it, eh?' said the master. 'Well, let's see how you write it. Write it out—legibly, please—a hundred and fifty times, and bring it to me to-morrow morning.' 'Oh, sir,' bemoaned the boy, and foolishly added, 'Shall I spell Joseph with an *f* or a *ph*?' 'Which d'you think is right in this case?' 'A *ph*, sir.' 'Well, to prevent any mistakes, do it a hundred and fifty times with a *ph*, and another hundred and fifty times with an *f*. And so that you don't miss any of the fun, while you're about it you can spell Plumb a hundred and fifty times with a *b* and a hundred and fifty times without. D'you think that will carry the joke far enough?' 'Oh, sir!' Well, you can imagine how unpopular that made me. But it wasn't my fault. All I'd said was 'Joseph Plumb.' "

"Well, Mr. Plumb, may I tell you about my troubles?" said Ronald.

"Please do," said Mr. Plumb.

"It's about the girl next door," began Ronald, and hesitated.

"The girl next door?" repeated Mr. Plumb.

"She's being a nuisance."

"Singing or something?" queried Mr. Plumb.

"Well, she did sing a few days ago, but it isn't that. No, she's threatened to follow me about."

"Follow you about? How d'you mean?"

"Well, she's got too fond of me. So I was proposing to move. She said that, if I did, she'd come with me."

"How old is the girl?"

"Seventeen."

"Well, the simplest way to stop that is to have her made a ward of court. Usually it's the parents who do that, to prevent the young lady going off with someone. But I can't see why the someone can't do it too. I've never heard before of such a case but I can't see any reason against it."

"She says that, if I do anything of that sort, she'll have a baby and say it's mine."

"Dear, dear," said Mr. Plumb. "May I ask—I mean—please forgive me—but I have to know the facts."

"Certainly not," said Ronald. "The idea is unthinkable. I look upon her more as a daughter."

"Then how can she make such a suggestion?"

"There's nothing to stop her from saying it, is there?" asked Ronald. "It would be quite untrue, but who's to know except her and me?"

"But she can't have a baby without someone."

"Of course not," said Ronald. "She says she'll just find someone, and then say it's me."

"How terrible," said Mr. Plumb, "and what a—"

"Bitch," said Ronald. "You're quite right, though it isn't altogether her fault. I ought to have realized what was happening. But I've become indispensable to her and she wants me desperately. I was awfully fond of her and I'm terribly sorry that this has happened. But it's quite intolerable. What can I do about it?"

"Well, you could get an injunction against her to stop her from pestering you."

"And suppose she retaliated by taking proceedings against me?"

"For what?"

"If she had a baby. I believe she's quite capable of getting some boy to do it. And he wouldn't want to show up afterward and claim the privilege of paying so much a week, would he?"

"No, I don't suppose he would," said Mr. Plumb.

"Well, I couldn't prevent her from taking proceedings against me, could I?" asked Ronald.

"You couldn't prevent her, but she'd lose the case."

"Why would she necessarily lose? It'd be word against word."

"She'd have to provide corroboration."

"What does that mean?"

"Something beyond her mere word."

"Such as?"

"An admission by you to some third party. Or a letter from you, or something of that sort."

"Well, she couldn't get anything like that."

"Then she'd lose the case."

"But it wouldn't be much fun having a case, even if I won it, would it?" said Ronald. "I'm over fifty. She's seventeen. People would be bound to talk. Would you trust me with your seventeen-year-old daughter after that?"

"No," said Mr. Plumb, "but I'm surprised you want any more."

"I don't, but I want to live a comfortable, carefree life without people whispering when they see me and so on. 'He's the man who had that case.' You know the sort of thing. People would hear about it sooner or later. And then another thing has occurred to me. This young woman is quite unscrupulous where I'm concerned. Suppose she got a girlfriend to come and lie about me?"

"In what way?"

"To provide this corroboration stuff you talked about."

"You mean she'd get a friend to say you'd admitted to her that you'd slept with the girl?"

"Something of the sort."

"That would be subornation of perjury, if she said it in court."

"I daresay, but she might find someone to do it. And in her present mood she'd certainly do it herself."

"Perhaps she'll change her mood."

"If only she would. But I doubt it. Anyway, tell me what I can do to prevent all this. There must be something. Why, if I were a parson or a schoolmaster, she could ruin me or do me the most tremendous harm."

"That does occasionally happen, I'm afraid. A false complaint can do a very great deal of harm to an innocent person. Fortunately it happens very rarely."

"That's no consolation if it's to happen this time. Now, you're a lawyer. I've told you the fix I'm in. Surely you can think of some way of avoiding the danger?"

"Well," said Mr. Plumb thoughtfully, "there *is* one thing you might do. It wouldn't prevent her from taking proceedings, but the knowledge that you'd done it might make her fear a prosecution for perjury if she took affiliation proceedings against you."

"What is it?"

"Well, you may not like the idea, but, if what you've told me is true, I think you'd be perfectly justified in doing what I suggest."

"What is it you suggest?"

"Have a tape recorder concealed in a room and get her to repeat the conversation you've told me about. You know, let her threaten you again as she did the other day. Then later, if she starts proceedings, let her and her solicitors hear the tape played over."

"What a wonderful idea," said Ronald. "I ought to have thought of it myself. If I'd had our last talk recorded, she couldn't possibly start anything against me once she knew of it. It would prove my innocence completely. I'm most grateful, Mr. Plumb. I'll get on with it at once. And I'll have several copies of the tape made, in case it is lost or destroyed, or she steals it."

"You'd better bring me one at once," said Mr. Plumb, "then it'll be absolutely safe. If I'm not in give it to my confidential clerk, Mr. Soames."

"Fine," said Ronald. "I can't thank you enough. I'll go straight off and arrange it."

So Ronald left Mr. Plumb's office in a much happier frame of mind. He had been so concerned for his own peace of mind, that it never even occurred to him that it was rather unpleasant to have to trap a girl to whom at one time he had been devoted. But, even if that thought had occurred to him, her outrageous behavior would amply have justified the action he was about to take.

He installed the machine, tested it for sound and then asked Jane to come and see him. She needed no pressing to come at once.

"Oh, Ronnieboy, how nice," she said. "I hoped you'd ask me soon. I haven't seen you for two whole days."

"I want to have a serious chat with you."

"Serious? Are you going to ask me to marry you? I'll say yes before you can ask it."

"No, Jane," said Ronald. "I want to talk to you about what you said the other day."

"About loving you, d'you mean?"

"That, and other things."

"Well, I always shall."

"But it was those other things you said you'd do. Say them again."

Jane said nothing for a moment, and then she said almost casually:

"When we were in bed, you mean?"

"What are you talking about?"

"The things I said I'd do for you. Why d'you want me to repeat them, Ronnieboy? Don't you believe me? Of course I'll do them for you. It's not as if there was anything wrong in them. They're quite natural."

"What d'you mean?" asked Ronald.

"You know what I mean," said Jane. "I promise. Next time we're in bed together as ever is. Cross my heart."

Ronald soon realized that Jane had sensed what he had been doing. So, after a few minutes, he dropped the pretense.

"At any rate," he said, "it shows you that I'm in earnest. I've seen my solicitor."

"Your solicitor!" said Jane. "What a fuss you do make. But I'm in earnest too, Ronnieboy. Why not be sensible and give in? You know, relax and enjoy it."

9

The Surrender

TWO DAYS LATER RONALD MADE A DECISION.

"I give in," he announced to a triumphant Jane. "It's all wrong. I know it. But, if your parents agree, I'll marry you."

"Ronnieboy!" said Jane. "Oh, Ronnieboy. How wonderful." Then she thought for a moment.

"You really do want me?" she asked. "I know I said I'd make you. But I wouldn't really want to, if you hated it."

"Of course I want it," said Ronald. "I just felt I shouldn't. That was all."

"Oh, how lovely," said Jane. "Darling, darling Ronnieboy. And you're going to be all my own forever—forsaking all others till death us do part."

"That's one of the things that worried me. I'm so much older than you. I hate the thought of your being alone."

"But it won't be for years and years, Ronnieboy. You'll live to be eighty at least."

"When I'm eighty you'll be under fifty."

"All the better to look after you. Oh, Ronnieboy, this is so wonderful. When shall we speak to Mummy and Daddy?"

"Whenever you like. I'll go this evening, if they'll be in."

"When will we be married?"

"That's usually for the lady to say."

"For me?"

"And your parents."

"How about tomorrow?"

"That's a bit soon. There'll have to be banns and things of that sort. And your parents may want us to wait a bit."

"Well, we don't have to wait for the actual ceremony, do we?"

"Not wait for what?"

"You know what I mean, Ronnieboy."

"Then certainly we shall wait," said Ronald. "I'm going to stand firm on that."

"But why? It can't do anyone any harm."

"Can't it?" said Ronald. "Suppose I died and you had a baby? That would be fine, wouldn't it?"

"I'm not bound to have a baby. We could provide against that."

"I dare say," said Ronald, "but the answer's still no. You'll have to be patient."

"It's all very well for you. You've had lots of women. You'll be my first, and I'm in a hurry. Let's go upstairs now."

"No, no, no," said Ronald. "I've relaxed and I'm going to enjoy it, but not till we're married. That's quite definite."

"How quickly can we be married?"

"That depends on your parents. They might want us to wait a year or two."

"A year or two!" said Jane. "We couldn't possibly wait that long. Not even a month or two. I want the soonest possible."

"Well, we must see."

"You won't change your mind?"

"Of course not."

Colonel and Mrs. Doughty were in that evening.

"Anything you want, Ronald," said the colonel, "or is this just a social call?"

"It's about Jane."

"Is she being a nuisance?"

"Not at all. I want to marry her."

"What!" said the colonel. "You're not serious?"

"I am."

"But she's only a child."

"I know. I've told her so."

"You could be her grandfather pretty well."

"Not quite," said Ronald. "But father, certainly."

"And she wants to marry you?"

"Apparently."

"Extraordinary. I don't know what to say. I'll call Marion."

After several calls Marion answered:

"Coming, dear."

"That may mean anything from two minutes to two hours," said the colonel. "Sometimes I have to remind myself that it's quite true she *is* coming. But *when*, that's the question. So you watch out, if you marry Jane. Always have a good book by you. Stops you from getting angry. I remember, after we were first married, I started to get annoyed. Used to shout back at her sometimes. Not good. Then a friend put me on to it. 'Always have a good book by you,' he said. 'Then waiting's nothing. You want to know who did the murder and hope she won't be down till you've found out.' I've made a point of it ever since. I always keep a book I've started and want to finish on that ledge. D'you know, sometimes I deliberately stop reading a book because I know it'll be a good waiting book. That's what I call them, waiting books. You won't mind how long she keeps you this way. D'you know, I really believe it would save some marriages. Things have to start somehow. And, if you can stop the first start, there may never be another. After all, there are few things more irritating than being kept waiting. I should be furious now if I weren't talking to you and hadn't a book to fall back on. But I have, you see. It's jolly good too. Wouldn't mind how long she kept me waiting, with that to read. Are you coming, dear?" he suddenly shouted. "Ronald's been here ages."

"Coming, dear."

"Don't mind me," said Ronald. "You read. I'll look at the paper."

"I think I will, old boy," said the colonel. "D'you know, I could feel the old gorge rising. Bad, that."

He picked up his waiting book and was soon engrossed in it, while Ronald looked at an evening paper but did not read it.

Half an hour later Marion arrived.

"Hope I haven't kept you," she said. "Hullo, Ronnie. You look serious."

"I should hope he did," said the colonel. "If a lunatic can be serious. He wants to marry Jane, and Jane wants to marry him. I don't know which is the bigger fool."

"To marry Jane!"

"I'm afraid so," said Ronald. "I know it's ridiculous, but she's awfully keen on the idea."

"But what about you?" asked Marion.

"Oh, I am too, of course," said Ronald, "but I realize it sounds pretty mad."

"It may sound mad," said Jane, coming in, "but it'll be such sweet madness."

"D'you realize," said Marion, "that, while you are still quite a young woman, he'll be spilling things down his waistcoat?"

"He does that now," said Jane, "but they still ask him to parties."

"Do I really?" said Ronald. "I'd no idea. You're joking?"

"Well, I've only noticed it recently. But there was a bit of avocado when we were all having dinner at the Myrtles'. And yesterday there was some yellow stuff—egg, no doubt. From breakfast."

"I must look into this," said Ronald.

"So, you see, I love him—avocado, egg and all. And I'll love mopping it up for him."

"But he may become a helpless invalid."

"I shall love wheeling him about."

"And then old men—well—I know it isn't very easy to say, but sometimes they start to smell."

"I say—" began Ronald.

"I'm sorry, Ronnie," said Marion, "but it's better that Jane should know now."

"He needn't if I keep him clean," said Jane, "and I shall love doing that."

"You talk of me as though I were some sort of animal."

"A darling, darling animal," said Jane.

"That's what you'd say if I were in a home for old horses."

"Have you really thought this thing out, Ronnie?" asked the colonel.

"Yes," said Ronald. "Like you, I thought first of all the things against it. And, of course, there are lots. But life is such a chancy thing, anyway. If I were twenty-two I might be drowned swimming. And anyone can be run over by a bus or killed in an accident."

"But if Jane were left a widow when you were a young man, she would marry again."

"So she can if I'm an old man. That's an advantage, actually. If I live another twenty-five years Jane will only be forty-two. And she'll be even more beautiful."

Jane squeezed his hand.

"I should never marry anyone else. And when you're dead, I'll just wait until I can join you. But that won't be for years. And just think of twenty-five years of heaven. Why, it's a life and a half. When can we be married?"

"Well, if you are quite determined on it," said the colonel, "I suppose in two or three years' time. What d'you say, Marion?"

"I waited till I was twenty-one," said Marion. "I didn't want to, but I did it."

"But I can marry at twenty-one whether you like it or not," said Jane. "And then I'd hate you for keeping us waiting. Surely you'd prefer me to love you, and say yes to next month?"

"Next month!" said Marion.

"We shan't feel any different next month, next year or next ten years. Why wait?" said Jane. "After all, it's not as though we were strangers. I've known him all my life."

"It's true that people do get married younger these days, but usually to people of their own age," said the colonel.

"Old Perkins married a girl of nineteen," said Jane.

"Nineteen isn't seventeen," said Marion. "Why not wait till then?"

"Because I don't want to," said Jane, and she looked at Ronald.

"Because we don't want to," he said, and she smiled happily at him.

"You shouldn't encourage the child, Ronnie," said Marion. "You're fifty-two, or whatever you admit to, and ought to know better. A girl in love at seventeen can't possibly see ahead sufficiently. You can."

"I can see ahead perfectly," said Jane. "I can see that, instead of my being a dried-up old woman when Ronnie gets a bit past it, I'll still be youngish and attractive and able to keep him young. That's the secret of life, to keep young. I'm going to keep us both young. It'll be just wonderful. Come on, you two—you must say yes."

"Give us time," said the colonel. "This is a great shock."

"How long d'you want?" asked Jane.

"A week," said the colonel, rather like a debtor asking for time to pay.

"Why d'you want so long?" asked Jane.

"I think a week's reasonable," said Ronald. He took Jane's hand. "I really do, darling," he added.

"I'm going to say 'obey,'" said Jane, "so I might as well start now. A week it shall be. Now come on, Ronnieboy," and she dragged Ronald out of the room.

"Come next door," she said, as soon as they were out of the room.

Once they were in Ronald's house Jane hugged him. "You are wonderful," she said. "Oh, Ronnieboy, they'll give in. And we shan't have to have any of that beastly court stuff."

"What court stuff?"

"I've been looking it up. If they refused, we could go to a magistrate. But it's much nicer like it is."

"You're very sure."

"I know Mummy and Daddy. Won't it be lovely to obey you, Ronnieboy. I'll do anything you say, anything at all. I'll start now so as to get into the habit. Tell me to take all my clothes off."

"I shall do nothing of the kind."

"Please."

"No."

"Well, just some of them. Then I can feel closer to you when I touch you."

"No. I'm all in favor of you obeying me. So let's start now, as you say. There's to be no funny business till we're married."

"But then it won't be funny business. It'll be all legal."

"Stolen fruit isn't the nicest, I assure you. It's much more comfortable being able to eat it without being frightened all the time that someone will come in and take it from you. I know. I've tried."

"But you've never been married, Ronnieboy, so you can't know both. Only the stolen kind. Did you love it? Did you ever get caught by an angry husband?"

"I could never love in fear," said Ronald.

"But I haven't a husband. What are you frightened of? Mummy and Daddy?"

"Well, they're one good reason for behaving ourselves. If they give their consent, they'll be trusting us. And it would be bad to start our life together by a breach of trust."

"Our life together," repeated Jane. "How wonderful it sounds."

"It'll be all the more wonderful for waiting," said Ronald.

"All right," said Jane. "But just once—for fun. To celebrate."

"No," said Ronald.

"I hate you," said Jane. "I hate-you-love-you-hate-you-love-you. The loves have it. But you might be nice to me. I only said just once."

"And then it would be just twice, and just three times, and then anyway we're being married so what does it matter?"

"Then if it were just once, and I gave you my solemn word of honor not to ask you again, you would do it?"

"No, I would not."

"You wouldn't take my solemn word of honor?"

"No," said Ronald, "in this case I wouldn't. You don't imagine Adam and Eve would have stopped at one apple if they'd had the chance of more? But, even if I did take your word, I'd still say we've got to wait."

"Don't you want to have me altogether?"

"Of course I do."

"You're too strong-minded. And you're strong-bodied too. Won't it be wonderful on our first night. You'll order me about, won't you? I'll be your woman, and you'll make me do whatever you want, won't you? And beat me, if I don't?"

Ronald looked almost sadly at her but she had turned her head and did not see.

"I would never beat you, Jane," he said. "Never."

"But I want you to, Ronnieboy. Just to show that I was yours and you could do whatever you liked to me."

"Love is kind, Jane. Real love, that is. Lust is something quite different."

"Then I've got both for you, Ronnieboy, so look out. I could eat you, or let you eat me. Let's eat each other. I wonder who'd have the last bite?"

"I was once told by a lawyer," said Ronald, "that if a man and woman are killed in an accident and there's no proof which of them died first, the woman is presumed by the law to have done so on the ground that women are weaker than men. But I've no doubt that it would be you who'd have the last bite."

"But I wouldn't want that, Ronnieboy. I'd be all alone. No, let's leave enough for another time. Just have an ear or something."

"Don't be beastly," said Ronald.

Meanwhile Colonel and Mrs. Doughty were discussing the matter.

"It's our fault," said the colonel. "We ought to have seen what might happen."

"I should, anyway," said Marion. "You haven't the imagination."

"I certainly have," said the colonel.

"Then why didn't you do something about it?"

"I should have."

"You didn't because you never thought about it."

"Well, if you thought about it, why didn't you do something about it?"

"I just don't know. Anyway, I'm Jane's mother and ought to have foreseen it."

"Well, I'm her father—and not such a blithering idiot as you'd make out."

"If you're not a blithering idiot, why did you let it happen?"

"It's no good bickering like this now, dear," said the colonel. "That won't do any good."

"What will do any good?"

"Suppose we speak to the parson?"

"We'll have to do that anyway—about the banns."

"You're going to agree just like that, then?" asked the colonel.

"I don't see what else we can do," said Marion. "Jane takes after you in some ways. She's as obstinate as a mule."

"I like that," said the colonel.

"Well, I don't," said Marion, "but I've had to live with it. And so will Ronald. I suppose he knows what he's letting himself in for? She'll have her own way or bust. That's one good thing, I suppose. Any young man she married would have the hell of a time. Ronald should be old enough to look after himself."

"You don't give Jane much of a character," said the colonel.

"I've never believed in shutting one's eyes to one's children's faults—or to one's husband's. After marriage, that is. Before then you try to pretend the faults don't exist."

"Well, you seem to have suffered me very patiently for a long time," said the colonel.

"And I hope I *shall* for a long time," said Marion, "but that doesn't blind me to the fact that you're an old fool. Or this would never have happened."

"I thought you said it was more your fault than mine."

"What does it matter whose fault it is? It's happened. And people will say we oughtn't to have allowed it."

"If it works out all right, I suppose that won't matter too much."

"But no one will know for years whether it's going to work out all right. It's now that we shall look such utter fools. Just imagine what everyone will say."

"What will they say?" said the colonel.

"That we were too wrapped up in our own affairs to bother about Jane."

"Well, it's true."

"That's most helpful."

"I was stating facts, not trying to be helpful," said the colonel.

"Don't you think it might be better to say something helpful?"

"What can I say that might be helpful?"

"That's what I want to know."

"Well, if we're going to give in, we'd better do so with a good grace. Have an engagement party and all that."

"That's the first sensible thing you've said. At any rate, that won't look as though Jane's in the family way already."

"Good Lord!" said the colonel. "I never thought of that. D'you think she is?"

"I wouldn't put it past her. But, to do him justice, I don't think Ronnie would. He's a decent enough chap."

"There were some very decent chaps in my regiment," said the colonel, "but they wouldn't have been above slipping into a convenient bed."

"With a girl of seventeen?"

"You've got a point there. She'd have had to have looked a bit older for one of our lot. I can't think of any of them as baby-snatchers. Possibly Halliwell. He was a bit of a dark horse. Shouldn't have been very surprised at anything *he* did."

"D'you mean Barry Halliwell? I thought he was rather charming."

"Too charming sometimes, I should say. Not with you, by any chance?"

"Don't be silly. But he was rather nice."

"Well, you were over seventeen, all right."

"Actually it was on my twenty-seventh birthday," said Marion.

"But about Jane," began the colonel, and then suddenly stopped. "What did you say?" he asked.

"Nothing."

"You said it happened on your birthday. What happened?"

"Nothing, I tell you."

"Then why did you say that it did? I never liked that chap. Are you solemnly sitting there and saying that twenty-seven years ago—"

"Twenty-six, please," put in Marion.

"If you say that, it's probably nearer thirty. But, whenever it was, are you telling me that Barry Halliwell—he of all people—"

"Yes, he did."

"Did what?" said the colonel.

"What I said."

"But you didn't say *what* he did."

"I didn't say he did anything."

"But you just said he did."

"Did what?" asked Marion.

"You said it was on your birthday."

"So it was."

"What was?"

"My birthday," said Marion.

"Your birthday was on your birthday, but what *happened* on your birthday?"

"I was born."

"What happened on what you are pleased at this distance of time to call your twenty-seventh birthday?"

"A lot of things, no doubt. I've forgotten most of them."

"What happened about Barry Halliwell?"

"Oh, him."

"Yes, him."

"You really want to know?"

"Yes, I do."

"After all this time?"

"Certainly."

"Well, as a matter of fact—it's hardly worth mentioning, really—"

"Let me be the judge of that."

"All right, then, as you're so curious. Barry Halliwell—I used to call him Bally Hally—d'you remember?"

"I do *not* remember. What did he *do*?"

"What did he do?"

"Yes, what did he do?"

"Well, actually, I don't remember what *he did*."

"D'you mean to say there were so many of them?"

"Don't be coarse. I can tell you what he said, if you want to know."

"I do want to know."

"Not his actual words, of course. I've forgotten those—you can't expect me to remember after all this time."

"What *did* he say?"

"I've told you, I can't remember his actual words."

"What was the substance?"

"The substance. Well, it was my birthday. Did I say my twenty-seventh?"

"You did."

"I expect I was right. Although one could be mistaken about the year, after all this time."

"What did he say?"

"Well, it was my birthday and he said I'd had a lot of presents. Was I feeling generous? Of course I said yes."

"Why 'of course'?"

"That's what I thought you'd like me to say. You wouldn't want a wife who said she was mean, would you?"

"It depends what she was asked to be generous with," said the colonel.

"Well, he asked me for a birthday kiss."

"And what did you do?"

"I don't remember if we had time. Someone came in."

"And that was all?"

"More than all. I've invented the whole thing. I didn't even call him Bally Hally. I thought it was quite bright to think of that on the spur of the moment."

10

The Party

IN THE END THE DOUGHTYS AND RONALD AND JANE agreed that they should give an engagement party within two or three weeks, but that the wedding should take place in six months. The only objecting party to the six months was Jane, but she was eventually placated by Ronald saying that during the six months they would see as much as possible of one another, going to theaters and concerts regularly and making day expeditions to the sea and country.

The invitations to the party naturally gave the neighborhood plenty to talk about. Most people disapproved of the marriage, but in a friendly way. The vicar, the Reverend Herbert Mattingly, took a different view.

"My dear Jane," he said, in one of his private talks with her, "I am not one of those who think there is a particular age for marriage. You are grown up, so far as the Church is concerned, and I am sure that God doesn't say that anyone is too young or too old for marriage. It is the attitude of mind which matters. There is no reason why you at seventeen should not approach your new life with the same reverence and understanding as someone much older. Unfortunately, there are people of all ages who have either a wrong attitude toward marriage or no attitude at all. In the former class are those who want to have sexual relations without subterfuge. Among this class are the people who still fear the already lessening social slur on those who live together, as it is said, in sin. Undoubtedly fornication is a sin, but to my mind it is far less of a sin than the blasphemy inherent in a marriage which is only undertaken by people to achieve a social status."

"I have sinned in my heart," said Jane. "I would sleep with Ronnie today, only he won't let me."

"He is a good man," said the vicar, "and you are a good girl."

"Good! After what I've just said?"

"Certainly, for having told me. There is no doubt that the natural desires of the flesh are hard to subdue, particularly in young, full-blooded people like you. You are lucky in marrying a man who can help you to keep these desires in the right perspective. There is nothing wrong whatever in wanting to have sexual relations with the man you are going to marry. On the contrary, it is right that you should. But this sexual urge is sometimes so strong that people forget that sex is only one part of marriage. Companionship is another. There are plenty of couples where the sex element can be strong but where there is no companionship. On the other hand, good companions may have no sexual urge toward each other. For marriage both are required."

"Oh, we have them—we have them," said Jane. "I love just being with Ronnie, talking to him, listening to him or just being silent with him."

"Then," went on the vicar, "fortified by love and companionship, you must set out in the world together to do all the good you can and, by your example rather than by the sort of lecture which I am giving you now—by your example spread Christian teaching throughout your world."

"You make me so happy, vicar," said Jane. "I've always loved talking to you but never more than now."

"That's because I'm saying what you want to hear, Jane. Being a parson is rather like being an advocate. If a barrister wants to convince a judge, he argues along with him rather than against him. If I had expressed horror at your wanting to sleep with Colonel Holbrook before you were married to him—"

But Jane interrupted.

"Do call him Ronnie, vicar," she said. "Forgive my interrupting but it sounds awful to talk of my wanting to sleep with Colonel Holbrook. That makes me think of a dreary old colonel with a big mustache."

"With Ronald, then," said the vicar. "If I'd been horrified at that, what chance would I have had with the rest of my sermon? We spend our lives sowing seeds, but to have any success, we must cultivate the ground first."

"Why d'you tell me the tricks of your trade, vicar?"

"Confidence begets confidence, Jane," said the vicar. "You were frank with me. I thought it good to be frank with you. And let me add to my frankness. I'm going to enjoy your party no end. And I shall sin then by eating and drinking too much. The desires of the flesh. I ought to subdue them, but I don't as much as I ought to. I wonder what God thinks when one day he hears me telling you it's wrong to sleep with your fiancé and the next day he sees me gourmandizing in your parents' house? Old hypocrite, he'll probably say. Well, we have to be to some extent. Even when in a sermon we assume to ourselves the sins of the congregation, that's hypocrisy of a kind. We do this and we don't that, I say, when I know very well that I don't do this and do do that. But to put it any other way would completely lose the sympathy of the congregation. You can imagine what people would think of a parson who told his congregation that he didn't sin half as much as they did. So we have to pretend we do. But perhaps after all it isn't pretense. We may sin more than we think we do. Now, run along, Jane. Behave yourself and God bless you."

When Mrs. Vintage heard the news, she was delighted.

"A party—good," she said.

The two barristers, Nicholas Shannon and Ernest Myrtle, reconciled themselves to dining under the same roof and both accepted. The judge wondered if he would be asked to make a speech and prepared for the occasion accordingly. Hazelgrove accepted, and so did the architect, surveyor and solicitor. Altogether Eleanor Gardens was to be well represented.

The evening arrived. Jane went to fetch Ronald.

"I wish it were our wedding night," she said. "Then I'd really enjoy it."

"Won't be long now," said Ronald.

"Not long!" said Jane. "Five whole months."

"It'll go quickly enough," said Ronald. "What shall we do next week?"

"Anything at all with you," said Jane.

"That won't do," said Ronald. "Don't forget that, as the Duke said in *Patience*, you can soon get tired of toffee. Now, what would you like? How about the South Downs? We'll end up in Westbourne and go to a supper dance."

"Lovely," said Jane.

The engagement dinner took a long time but eventually the port was served and the judge was delighted when Colonel Doughty whispered to him. He rose almost immediately.

"Ladies and gentlemen," he began, "I don't know how many of you were told that there would be no speeches. Well, I wasn't. And I'm glad of it. Some of you may think, and possibly say out of my hearing, that I like the sound of my own voice. Quite right. I do. There are few things that give me more pleasure than being asked to speak for nothing. When I was at the bar they paid me to speak. When I was on the bench they paid me to keep quiet. At least that's how I understood it. Some judges, I believe, take an opposite view, but I disagree with them. It wouldn't be a bad idea, don't you think, to ration judges in their words, and deduct from their salary so much a thousand words over the allotted number. That would certainly shorten judgments and summing-ups, and lessen interruptions. But, to return to the point, I am always pleased to speak but never more so than on this very happy occasion. Some people may think that Jane is a bit young to run the risks of matrimony. I don't pretend I'm not one of them. Everybody wants everything too much and too soon these days. But, all the same, if she's prepared to take the risk, and Ronald is ready to take it with her, why then good luck to them both, and may the devil take the hindmost."

There was considerable applause at this stage, but the judge did not sit down.

"I couldn't possibly let you off as easily as that," he went on, "and I can't believe that our host didn't expect me to go on for at least ten minutes. And that, I may say, is about my minimum. That's only fifteen or sixteen hundred words. I must say that it's nice these days to have a formal engagement and a formal party. For one thing it means another party in a few months' time. And that reminds me that I mustn't say all the things that would be more appropriate for a wedding. Jane and Ronnie have lived next door to each other all her life, and if this isn't a guarantee that they must know a good deal about each other by now, I don't know what is. And that to my mind is a very great point in their favor. Ronnie must have seen Jane at her worst many times. Every prospective marriage partner should see the other with his or her parents for prolonged periods. For a short time a young woman can be on her best behavior with her parents, but not for long. Sooner or later she will let fly and show what she's really like. That's when her ardent suitor should be around. To hear what the sweet innocent child calls her parents. Ronnie must have heard Jane lots of times. Unfortunately, Jane hasn't been able to see Ronnie in the same circumstances. But she must think what she's like with her own parents and try to remember that Ronnie was probably no better with his. In other words, as long as they know that neither of them is an angel—though admitting that Jane usually looks like one—as long as they know this, they should come to no harm. I ask you all to rise and drink to the health and happiness of Jane and Ronnie, and wish them well—first over the next five months and then over the rest of their lives."

The judge sat down.

"Not too long, I hope," he whispered to his neighbor.

"Delightful," was the reply. "I don't know how you think of such apt things to say on the spur of the moment."

A few minutes later Ronald stood up.

"Thank you very much, Sir William and everyone, for wishing Jane and me well. I know that some of you, like the judge, think Jane is a little young for me. I thought so at one time. But I've been convinced to the contrary. Sir William is right when he says that Jane and I know each other very well, and, if I may say so, right too when he says how important that is as a basis for a happy marriage. This will be my first venture. And I hope my last. I might have been married several times in the past—don't worry, I wasn't —if I hadn't wanted to be sure that I should be marrying the right person. Fortunately I saw the light, or the lady in question saw it—it doesn't matter which—before there was even a tacit engagement. So here I am, as much a new boy as Jane will be a new girl. Well, almost as much, anyway. And I look forward to learning with her how a married couple should behave. Only experience can tell us. In the Army during the last war they used to have battle schools and all sorts of things like that, where they tried to reproduce the atmosphere of a real battle. Of course it couldn't be done. If anyone was hurt or killed during any such experiments, it caused a feeling of intense anger. One expects to be killed by one's enemies, not by one's friends. Moreover, no one can tell how a single man or a body of troops will behave in battle until they have been in actual battle. It is only experience of actual fighting that makes a good soldier. However, the powers that were thought that battle schools were a good thing and they killed off and wounded a number of people in the process. No one has, however, sought to introduce marriage schools. They would certainly be more fun than battle schools, and the wounds which some of the students might receive would be far less unpleasant. They might even be pleasant. But I fear such an experiment would hardly be practical, and Jane and I must learn by going into action. I look forward to the day when the vicar sounds the 'Charge,' as much as I hope Jane does. There will be no withdrawal or surrender. We will fight to the last man. But perhaps I'm pushing my metaphor too far. It would be more accurate to say that we shall each surrender to the other. No one can prophesy the future with accuracy. Not even the scientists. But, with my parents-in-law and all our friends to support us, I personally believe that we shall start our life together with as much chance of success as the many happy families we know living in this neighborhood. I rather think that, when people complain of the divorce rate, they are inclined to overlook the happy-marriage rate, which is still considerable. I profoundly hope and firmly believe that Jane and I will add one more to that number."

He sat down amid much applause and Jane kissed him.

Altogether it was a happy and successful evening, and most people agreed that the intended marriage was not perhaps such a bad idea after all.

A few days later Ronald and Jane went to Westbourne.

Mr. Plumb, the solicitor, going home that night by train, was reading the evening paper. When he came to the stop-press he said aloud, "Good gracious!" A few heads turned to look at him and he did not speak his next thoughts. But he said to himself, "Well, that solves his problem, anyway." As he folded his paper, however, before getting out, he added, "Or does it?"

11

❀

A Matter of Confidence

IN THE MORNING MR. PLUMB READ THE DETAILS. Jane had fallen
to her death near Spike Point, the headland just outside Westbourne. A distraught Ronald had rushed for help but she had been
killed instantly by the fall.

"Poor girl," said Mr. Plumb aloud to his wife. "But how odd."

"Who's poor, and what's odd?" asked Mrs. Plumb.

"Oh, nothing, dear. A wretched girl fell down a cliff and was
killed."

"Poor thing," said Mrs. Plumb. "How old was she?"

"Only seventeen," replied Mr. Plumb. "It says here that she had
just got engaged."

"What a tragedy. Poor young man. How awful for him."

"He isn't so young, as a matter of fact. Old enough to be her
father."

"Was he killed too?"

"No. It says here that they were at the edge of the cliff just after
dusk. Apparently the man turned away and then he heard the girl
cry out and just saw a bit of her as she fell down the cliff."

"What a terrible experience. I wish you hadn't told me. Not at

68

breakfast. I shall be thinking of them all day."

"I rather wish I hadn't read it," said Mr. Plumb. "There'll be an inquest, of course. I wonder what I ought to do?"

"Why should you do anything?"

"Curiously enough, the man had consulted me."

"What about?"

Mr. Plumb did not answer immediately. Then:

"It was confidential," he said.

"But why should you be involved?" asked his wife.

"I suppose I'm not really. But it's certainly very odd."

"You keep on saying that. What's odd?"

"I'm sorry, my dear. I can't tell you."

"You shouldn't have said it, then. You're always doing that. Saying something which makes me want to know more, and then going back into your shell and saying it's confidential. If it was confidential, you shouldn't have mentioned it."

"You're quite right, dear. I shouldn't have. I'm sorry."

"Well, please don't do it again. You've upset me for the rest of the day telling me about the poor girl, and you've irritated me at the same time by being all mysterious about it."

"I've said I'm sorry," said Mr. Plumb. "And I really am. Now I must go to the office. Forgive?"

"All right," said Mrs. Plumb, "but I still wish you hadn't told me."

"And I still wish I hadn't read it."

Mr. Plumb was a solicitor of the highest integrity. A number of good lawyers cannot restrain themselves from discussing difficult cases with their wives, usually without mentioning names. But for Mr. Plumb the rules of his profession were sacred and, much as he would have liked to talk over the matter with his sensible wife, he would not do so. But he had to get advice from someone about his problem. On the way to the office he called on a colleague of his, Stanley Frensham, whose views he respected and who was as trustworthy as he was himself.

"Stanley," he said, "I want your advice. Please treat what I'm going to say in the strictest confidence. I've got a problem. Later on you may guess what it is, but please keep it absolutely to yourself."

"Of course."

"Suppose a woman came to you for advice about divorcing her husband, and made it plain that she desperately wanted a decree. And suppose the evidence wasn't all that satisfactory and you advised her that, although a petition might succeed, it might not. And suppose some weeks afterward you read that your client's husband had been accidentally drowned while sailing with his wife. Would you feel you had to do anything about it and, if so, what?"

"The suggestion being that you were possibly the only independent person to know either that it was not an accident or else that it was a very happy coincidence for the wife?"

"Exactly."

"Presumably they were reconciled, to be sailing together. I imagine they were alone?"

"Well, if a woman badly wanted a divorce in order to marry someone else, and if she were told she hadn't sufficient grounds, she might pretend to be reconciled in order to be able to get her husband into a place where she could kill him and pretend it was an accident."

"And, of course, when you told her that the grounds weren't very strong, she might know that even what she'd told you wasn't the truth—so that a divorce was out of the question."

"Quite. Well, what would you do if you read about the accident?"

"It's not easy, is it? Everything she said to you was said in absolute confidence. No court could make you repeat it. Of course, if she'd come to ask you how to murder her husband, that would be different. No confidence would attach to such a conversation."

"But she didn't. For all we know, when she came to me, she'd never even thought of killing her husband. She came simply to find out if there was a legitimate way of getting rid of him. Supposing I went to the police; all I could say would be that she had consulted me. I couldn't say what about or even hint what it was about. So, for all the police would know, it might have been about buying a house, making a will, or a hundred other completely innocuous things."

"The fact that you went to the police at all might make them wonder. Why should a solicitor go to the police when a man's been drowned just because his wife had consulted him about claiming damages from a hairdresser or the like? It would certainly make them sit up and take interest."

"Are you entitled to make the police sit up and take interest in your client because of something confidential which she's said to you?" asked Mr. Plumb.

"If the mere fact of her calling on you could be a link in the chain of a crime, then I think that you not only could but should disclose it to the police. But, if it is only a link if you can go on to say what she consulted you about, then I don't think you've a duty to report the matter."

"But *if* there's been a crime—I repeat, *if* there's been a crime, because after all it may have been a genuine sailing accident—but *if* there's been a crime, surely we have some duty to the public as well as to our client. Haven't we?"

"Well, as I said before, anything done or said in pursuance of a proposed crime is, of course, unprivileged and you must report it. But, if what you were told was *not* told to you in pursuance of a crime, I doubt if you may tell anyone about it, even though its disclosure would show a motive for the crime. One can think of all sorts of cases. Supposing an employer consulted you as to what notice it was necessary to give to an employee, and made it plain that he wanted to get rid of him at the earliest possible moment. You surely couldn't repeat that conversation to anyone without your client's consent—even if ten days later the employee was found murdered."

"You say 'without your client's consent,' " said Mr. Plumb. "So at any rate I could ask the woman if she would agree to my informing the police?"

"And if she refused?"

"I suppose that then I couldn't do anything about it."

"But at least you'd have salved your own conscience by doing what you could to assist the public—I mean by asking your client for permission to tell the police."

"But, if she refused, that would in a way make matters worse for me, because it would increase the suspicion in my own mind," said Mr. Plumb.

"But the woman might be justified in refusing. 'It would look so bad,' she could say. 'I'm completely innocent in this matter but it would make people talk, wouldn't it? I've a clear conscience. Why should I create trouble for myself?' And she's got a good point there. People are only too ready to suspect other people. So, are you entitled to put your client in that dilemma? If you ask for permission to tell the police, what in effect you say to her is this: 'If you refuse I may suspect you; if you agree, your neighbors may.' A nice position in which to place your own client who's paid you for your advice. And, don't forget, it may just have been a coincidence. There are plenty of sailing accidents. And you do this to salve your own conscience."

"It's very worrying," said Mr. Plumb.

"A solicitor may often be worried by things like this, but that's one of the troubles of the job. Suppose a man came into my office and consulted me about a murder. 'I've done it,' he says. 'What counsel d'you recommend for the job?' Suppose later on he withdraws his instructions from me and goes to another solicitor. Later I read that he pleaded not guilty, relied upon an alibi and was acquitted. There's nothing I can do about it, is there? I know a guilty man has been acquitted, but people could never safely consult a lawyer unless what they said was absolutely confidential. And the same thing would apply before he was acquitted. I could read in the papers that he was putting up a defense which I knew was completely false, and I'd just have to comfort myself by saying that, in the long run, it's better that such a thing can happen occasionally and that people can consult lawyers without any fear that their confidences will ever be disclosed without their consent."

"So you say," said Mr. Plumb, "that I should do absolutely nothing. I could legally go to my client and ask for permission to inform the police, but even that is undesirable."

"Now that I come to think of it, it may be more than undesirable. Suppose the lady did murder her husband. As her one-time solicitor, are you going in effect to advise her to make a present to the police of evidence against her?"

"Yes, I see that," said Mr. Plumb. "So what you say in effect is this: If she's guilty, I myself would be guilty of a breach of my duty to her as a lawyer if I advised her to create evidence against herself. If she's innocent, what have I got to worry about?"

"That's about it."

"Well," said Mr. Plumb, "let's hope it was an accident."

"And, after all," said Mr. Frensham, "it's one thing to want to divorce your husband, quite another thing to kill him, or even to think of it."

"True enough," said Mr. Plumb, "but all the same I wish she hadn't been so frantic about getting a divorce."

"But people do change their minds, and who knows the way a wife's mind may work, or a husband's for that matter? The permutations of action and inaction, play and interplay, in domestic relations are incalculable. A woman may hate one day and love the next. Indeed in some cases the intensity of the new love is greater because of the former hate. The husband may have hurt her pride bitterly just before she came to see you. When she goes back to the house he gives her a dozen roses and says he's sorry. He may have committed more matrimonial offenses than there were roses or he may not, but the breakup of the marriage may have been averted—at any rate for the moment—by the husband's contrition. Now, you must know plenty of cases where that has happened."

"I don't do much divorce work, as a matter of fact."

"Well, I do. And I must admit that I get more personal pleasure out of hearing my client has made it up, than from a hotly contested ten-day case. Wouldn't do for the practice, though, if they made it up too often. But they do, you know, and sometimes your frantic angry client may have made it up with her husband the next day and gone for a sailing holiday to celebrate."

"Then what a tragedy for them that, after their troubles and their reunion, one of them should die by accident," said Mr. Plumb.

"There are plenty of tragedies and plenty of coincidences in life."

"I know. But as a lawyer I don't like coincidences. I know they happen, but seldom when someone would like them to happen. How many husbands or wives who would like to get rid of their partners have found them dead in bed from natural causes? How many unwanted husbands or wives have fallen accidentally out of a train or into a well? Murder or suicide, yes, but accident I find very hard to swallow."

"You think that problems are solved more often by one of Kai Lung's methods than by coincidence?" asked Mr. Frensham.

"Kai Lung?" queried Mr. Plumb.

"Yes. Don't you know your Kai Lung? It went something like this: 'There are few problems in life which cannot be cured by suicide, a bag of gold or by thrusting a despised adversary over a cliff during the hours of darkness.'"

"Good God!" said Mr. Plumb. "Say that again."

His friend repeated the quotation.

"Well, I'm damned," said Mr. Plumb.

"Why on earth?" asked Mr. Frensham.

"Nothing," said Mr. Plumb. "Just another coincidence."

12

Comforters

THE TRAGEDY CAST A GLOOM OVER ELEANOR GARDENS and everyone, even the mysterious Mr. Sinclair, offered comfort to Ronald and Jane's parents.

The vicar was one of the first to call on Ronald.

"There's nothing I can say to help," he began. "You know how deeply we all feel for you."

"Everyone is very kind," replied Ronald.

"Can I do anything?"

"Well," said Ronald, "would you be able to make the funeral arrangements? The Doughtys would like her buried here and for you to conduct the service. But there's all the business about bringing her back. And, of course, it can't be till after the inquest."

"Leave it to me," said the vicar. "Just fix the day and time with Jane's parents, and I'll do the rest."

"You're very good."

"It's nothing. I wish there were some way to comfort you." There was silence for a short time. "Could you give me any idea—" the vicar began.

"The inquest is on Friday," said Ronald. "As a matter of fact,

I'm expecting the coroner's officer to be here any moment. There's the bell. Perhaps that's him. Excuse me."

Ronald went to the door. It was not the coroner's officer. It was Mr. Sinclair. The vicar excused himself, and Mr. Sinclair sat down.

"I'm sorry that my first call on you should be in such circumstances," he said, "but I read of the tragedy and felt I must call to offer my condolences."

"How very kind of you."

"It's nothing. To tell you the truth, I may have come as much for my own sake as for yours. I can't get your tragedy out of my mind. It's too terrible."

"Thank you," said Ronald.

"To have been so close to her and yet to have been unable to save her must be one of your worst thoughts. I know that it's mine. It goes round and round my head. Why wasn't I a foot closer to her? Why didn't I look round at that moment? Why did she have to go so close to the edge? Why didn't I stop her? And a hundred other things."

"I have to try not to think of it," said Ronald.

"But unfortunately for you," said Mr. Sinclair, "they'll make you think of it. I'm thinking of the inquest. These lawyers. They don't consider other people's feelings. All they're after, they say, is the truth. The truth! What do they know about the truth! And they don't mind how many people they hurt in trying to find it out. I can't tell you how I sympathize."

"I'm expecting the coroner's officer at any moment," said Ronald.

"Then I won't intrude any longer," said Mr. Sinclair. "Thank you for seeing me. I felt I should go mad if I didn't talk to you. Somehow or other I keep on identifying myself with you. I see myself on that cliff, and that poor little girl so close—but not quite close enough. Or was it that you could have put out a hand but didn't know it was needed? Forgive my asking you, but my mind goes round and round with the thought of it. If only—if only, I keep on saying to myself."

"Forgive me, Mr. Sinclair," said Ronald, "but it's I who have lost Jane, not you."

"I'm a blundering idiot," said Mr. Sinclair. "I'd no business to have asked you all these questions. How they must hurt. You may even have thought that I was suggesting that you might have saved her. I am so very sorry. I came here to offer sympathy and all I do is rub the wound. Please forget all I've said and just accept my deepest sympathy on your terrible loss. Good-bye."

"Good-bye," said Ronald, and showed Mr. Sinclair to the door. As he did so the coroner's officer arrived. Ronald took him into the sitting room.

"I'm very sorry to have to trouble you, sir," the officer began, "but I'm sure you'll understand that I'll have to ask you quite a lot of questions."

"Of course," said Ronald. "I fully understand."

"May I first of all express my deepest sympathy? I understand you were engaged to the young lady."

"That is so. We were to be married in about five months."

"How long have you known her, sir?"

"All her life."

"Then you knew her well?"

"Very well indeed."

"Was she an adventurous young lady, as you might say?"

"She was full of life, if that's what you mean."

"Did you go for many walks together?"

"Oh, yes, many."

"Did she sometimes run on ahead or up the side of a slope, rather like a dog does, if you'll forgive my putting it that way, sir?"

"It's a very good way of putting it, officer. Yes, she did. And then sometimes she'd shout to me to join her. She'd say she'd found something or there was a wonderful view."

"Yes, I follow, sir. I take it she was not afraid of heights."

"No, not a bit. She enjoyed them. More than I did, I may say."

"Are you afraid of heights, sir?"

"Not very, but sometimes she'd shout to me to come and look down somewhere. Over a cliff or something. Sometimes I felt a bit squeamish, but I didn't like a little girl to think I was frightened. So I usually went."

"Where had you been just before the accident?"

"Just strolling along the cliff. Then she suggested sitting down for a bit."

"And did you?"

"Yes."

"For how long?"

"Not very long."

"Were you both tired?"

"No, not very. Why?"

"I just wondered why she suggested sitting down," said the officer.

"How much of this has to come out in court?" asked Ronald.

"Well, sir, everything that's got anything to do with the cause of death. But the coroner's very careful not to hurt people's feelings if he can avoid it."

"Well, it's just this. We sat down because she wanted me to make love to her."

"I see. And did you, sir? I'm sorry to have to ask the question."

"No. I kissed her, but that was all."

"Was she annoyed at this at all, sir?"

"Not exactly annoyed. We'd talked about the matter on other occasions and—but really, officer, I don't see what this has to do with the case. Good Lord! You're not suggesting she may have thrown herself over the cliff in a fit of pique."

"I hadn't thought of that, sir."

"Well, I can assure you that nothing of the kind happened," said Ronald. "She wasn't pleased at my saying we would wait, but she was intensely happy and looking forward to our marriage. The thought of suicide is quite ridiculous—out of the question."

"I quite agree, sir, but with death of this kind, suicide being a not uncommon cause, we have to rule it out. And you say that she was very happy and couldn't possibly have wanted to take her own life?"

"Couldn't possibly—unless she suddenly went out of her mind."

"You've no reason to think she did? A brainstorm or something?"

"Well, she'd never had one before, as far as I know."

"What exactly happened?"

"Well, we were lying about ten yards from the edge. She got up and said something about it being a lovely evening and she was going to look over the edge."

"Did she suggest you should come too?"

"Yes, she did."

"What did she say?"

"Her actual words?"

"If you remember them, sir."

"Something like 'Come along, Ronnieboy'—that's what she called me—'Come along, Ronnieboy.'" As he repeated 'Ronnieboy,' Ronald half choked and had to be silent for a few moments.

"I'm sorry it's so very painful for you, sir," said the officer. Ronald said nothing. After a short time he went on:

"I said I didn't want to or something like that. I was in fact a bit scared to look over."

"Usually you overcame the feeling, sir, but this time you didn't?"

"That's about it. I just said I was very comfortable where I was and told her to be careful."

"Were you frightened of her falling over?"

"Not in the least. I'd often seen her do that kind of thing. She was as steady as a rock."

"And then what happened, sir?"

"I took my eyes off her. I think I was going to light a cigarette. I suddenly heard her say 'Oh.' Not very loud. I looked up and she was gone. I just saw a bit of her going down over the edge."

"What part of her did you see?"

"I can't really be sure. It may have been her head, but I was so shocked I can't be sure. I ran to the edge, threw myself down and looked. She bounced on something and then went out of my sight. I rushed for help."

"Then it's quite clear, sir, that from where you were lying you couldn't have saved her?"

"I was ten yards away."

"Quite, sir. From where you were you couldn't have touched her nor she you?"

"Of course not."

"I'm sorry, sir. It must be very distressing for you, sir, but the coroner has to clear up every possibility."

"What d'you mean by every possibility?"

"There's no need to go into that in a case like this, sir."

"If you want to ask me whether I pushed her over, I wish you would," said Ronald.

"You were ten yards away, sir. So you couldn't have."

"I'd much prefer you to have asked me straight out," said Ronald.

"I'm sorry, sir. Most people wouldn't. Indeed, sir, I could imagine that many people, including yourself, sir, might have been very hurt, if not very angry, if I'd asked such a question in a case like this. So I asked it in a different way, sir, if you follow me, so as to be as helpful as possible. I'm sorry if I've offended you, sir."

"You haven't, officer. It's my fault," said Ronald. "But perhaps you can understand that some people—and I'm one of them— prefer the direct question. It's the waltzing around it which one doesn't like."

"I quite follow, sir, and I hope you understand my point of view, sir. People are so different. Mine's not altogether an easy job. I've got to try to sort out the facts without hurting people's feelings, if I can avoid it. And these cliff deaths are quite a problem. There are quite a lot of them all round the country. Most of them are pure accidents, but there are suicides and—" The officer didn't complete the sentence.

"And murder," said Ronald. "There you go again."

"I'm sorry, sir. Yes, there's accident, suicide and murder. And whichever it is, we've got to try to find out who's responsible. The local council may be involved. Is the cliff dangerous? Should it have been roped off? Should there be more warning signs? Has it been crumbling? Is it slippery? And so on. Westbourne is a holiday resort and unnatural deaths don't do us any good. So when we get one, we do what we can to prevent others. And finding out exactly why the one occurred is the first step. Well, I think I've asked you all I want to know, sir. For the moment, anyway. Thank you very much, sir. And once again please accept my deep sympathy."

When the coroner's officer had gone Ronald went back to his sitting room and sat in an armchair looking straight in front of him. He was still sitting there in the same position an hour later when the bell rang.

13

The Inquest

IT WAS MR. HIGHCASTLE AND A CLIENT. Mr. Highcastle was in great good humor.

"I've brought Mr. Samson," he said. "He's already taken a fancy to your house from the outside. I'm sorry not to have given you more notice, but I hoped you'd be in and I took a chance. May we come in?"

"I don't think I want to sell," said Ronald.

"But really, sir," said Mr. Highcastle, "you told me that it was an urgent matter and that you must get out as quickly as possible. In consequence, I've taken a great deal of trouble to try to sell it for you. Indeed, I've incurred quite an amount of expense in the process, not to mention time and trouble. And I ought to warn you, sir, houses like these are not going to improve in price. I don't know if that's what you're thinking. I warned you before that some owners are very foolishly holding back. I wouldn't recommend you to do the same. And Mr. Samson here is a serious buyer. That is so, is it not, Mr. Samson?"

"It is indeed," said Mr. Samson. "And might I add, if it's of any help, that's to say if you haven't finally made up your mind, I should complete quickly and I don't need a mortgage?"

"There you are, sir," said Mr. Highcastle. "What did I tell you? You may regret this change of mind, sir, very much indeed. Are you quite sure that you don't want to sell?"

"I'm afraid so," said Ronald.

"Well, it's really too bad, Mr. Holbrook. You've given me no notice whatever, and you've put my firm to a lot of expense; we've advertised your house and lost no end of time about it. I shall really have to consider sending you in an account."

"If you'll tell me what your out-of-pocket expenses are I shall be pleased to refund them. I don't remember actually asking you to advertise, but I'll certainly pay the cost of the advertisements."

"Actually there's no charge for them," said Mr. Highcastle, a little uncomfortably. "They were in our front window."

"I see," said Ronald. "Well, what are the other expenses you were talking about?"

"Well, I've brought Mr. Samson in the firm's car."

"Fair enough," said Ronald. "How many miles is it?"

"It isn't worth talking about," said Mr. Highcastle.

"Well, it's you who've talked about out-of-pocket expenses."

"What about my time? That's worth five or ten guineas an hour."

"And how many hours have you spent on my business?"

"Three or four certainly."

"But surely," said Ronald, "if Mr. Samson had bought the house you would have made two or three hundred pounds' commission. Three or four hours' work isn't bad for that. Isn't that the risk you take?"

"I can only say that it's very unfair treatment. We have to live like anyone else."

"I'm sorry," said Ronald, "but it's because my fiancée has been killed in an accident that I've changed my mind."

"Why didn't you say so, sir?" said Mr. Highcastle. "I'm extremely sorry, very sorry indeed. Please accept my deepest sympathy. I shouldn't dream of sending in an account in the circumstances. I'm sorry I mentioned it. We won't intrude on your grief any more. Should you at any time want to sell the house, sir, please consider my firm entirely at your service."

Mr. Highcastle and Mr. Samson left and Ronald went back to

his chair. He thought about the early days with Jane. How he had loved the child. He thought of the games which they used to play together, their walks, their going to church. He was near to tears when Colonel Doughty called to talk about the funeral.

A week later the inquest was held at the Coroner's Court in Westbourne.

"Members of the jury," said the coroner, "this is an inquiry into the circumstances in which a young woman, Jane Doughty, aged seventeen, met her death. She fell down a cliff at Spike Point at about eight o'clock in the evening. Her fiancé, Colonel Holbrook, was with her and will tell you how she came to fall. After you've heard his account you may like to visit the site."

Shortly afterward Ronald gave evidence and in substance repeated what he had told the coroner's officer.

"Colonel Holbrook," asked the coroner, "do you think that you would be able to point out to the jury the place from where she fell?"

"I expect so," said Ronald, "though I may not be able to place it exactly."

Later, after the coroner and jury had been with Ronald to Spike Point, Ronald went back in the witness box.

"Colonel Holbrook," said the coroner, "there does not appear to be any evidence that the dead girl slipped, does there?"

"No," said Ronald. "I feel sure that I took you to the approximate place from where she fell."

"So that, even if you were mistaken by twenty yards, there was no place at the edge where there appeared to be a slippery patch or where the cliff had given way at the edge."

"That is so," said Ronald.

"So the probability is," said the coroner, "don't you think, that she either became dizzy or overbalanced?"

"I think that must be so."

"Had she ever shown signs of dizziness before?"

"Never to my knowledge. Had she been that sort of girl, I wouldn't have let her go so near."

"And I gather that she was quite used to standing on heights and even sometimes balancing on a rock quite precariously?"

"That is so," said Ronald. "She was a very well-balanced girl."

"You've already told us that there was no reason you knew for her to take her own life," said the coroner. "Are you quite sure of that?"

"Absolutely. She had every reason to live."

"You hadn't had a tiff or anything of that kind just before she fell?"

Ronald hesitated very slightly.

"No," he said, "we never had what you call 'tiffs.'"

"Call it a disagreement, even a slight one."

Ronald said nothing.

"Had you had a disagreement?"

"No, we hadn't."

The coroner looked at his notes. "I'm sorry to ask you this, but is it possible that she wanted you to be more amorous than you thought right at that stage?"

This was too much for Colonel Doughty. "Really, sir," he said, "that is a horrible suggestion, and what on earth has it got to do with the case?"

"Colonel Doughty," said the coroner, "I am extremely sorry for you and your wife in your tragic loss, but, if you wish to remain in court, you must not interrupt."

"You insult the dead, sir," said the colonel. "How can you expect me to keep quiet at that?"

"I have no intention of insulting anyone," said the coroner. "I have a duty to perform and that is to assist the jury to arrive at a conclusion as to the cause of your daughter's death."

"Well, I'm sure the jury can do that without such questions," said the colonel.

The foreman of the jury then stood up. "Forgive my interrupting, sir," he said, "but the jury do not want that question to be answered."

"Thank you," said the colonel.

"Very well," said the coroner. "I won't pursue the matter. Tell me, Colonel Holbrook, what is your view as to the cause of her fall?"

"I can only say what you have said, sir. She must have either become dizzy or overbalanced. I'm quite sure that it was accidental and that she didn't have a brainstorm or anything like that. And

I'm quite sure she didn't suddenly have a fatal fascination to throw herself off, like it is said some people do with tube trains. She wasn't that sort of girl. She was absolutely normal."

Ronald was not asked many further questions, and the coroner summed up.

"Members of the jury," he said, "it is now your duty to examine the possibilities of this case and come to a conclusion on the matter. When a person falls off a cliff it may be due to one of several causes: murder, manslaughter, suicide or accident. In my view there is no evidence whatever which would entitle you to bring in a verdict of murder. You may perhaps wonder why I mentioned manslaughter. Such a verdict could be justified where people were playing about recklessly at the edge of a cliff and one of them fell over as a result. Once again, I must tell you that there is no evidence whatever that this young woman met her death through dangerous horseplay. The only evidence—and it is upon the evidence that you have to record your verdict—the only evidence is that Colonel Holbrook and the young woman were lying on the ground some ten yards from the edge of the cliff when the girl got up and went to the edge, and then fell. If those are the facts, no kind of responsibility, moral or legal, can attach to Colonel Holbrook. I say 'If those are the facts,' but I ought to point out to you that you have no evidence of any other facts. If, for some reason of which I cannot think, you decided that you did not believe a word which Colonel Holbrook has said, that would not replace his evidence by other evidence. It would simply leave you with no credible evidence about the matter. In those circumstances, unless the physical facts were such that they themselves raised an inference that Colonel Holbrook was responsible for the girl's death, you still would have no right to find a verdict that he was in any way blameworthy. Now, the physical facts raise no such inference. In the result, I tell you that, whatever your view of Colonel Holbrook's evidence, you cannot, on the evidence, return a verdict implicating him in any way. In saying this I want to make it plain that I am not suggesting for a moment that Colonel Holbrook should not be believed. As far as I could judge, he gave his evidence well. The remaining possibilities, then, are suicide or accident. Once again I have to tell you that there is wholly insufficient evidence to justify a verdict of suicide. The evidence is that this was a normal, healthy girl with every reason for living. She was going to be married shortly. Why should she take her life except as a result of a brainstorm? As to that, there is no evidence that she was a person who was likely to have a sudden attack of that kind. If there had been more evidence to suggest that the girl threw herself down, you would have to consider the state of her mind at the time. Once again, as far as the evidence goes, this young woman was entirely sane. But, as I have said, there is no need for you to return a verdict on that matter, as you cannot properly find that the girl threw herself over the cliff. It is quite true that suicide is no longer a crime in law. But at the lowest it is a very serious matter to take one's own life, and before a court should say that this has been done it must have substantial evidence at the least that suicide was the probable cause of the tragedy. There remains accident and, as far as I can see, you have no alternative but to say that this was an accident, pure and simple, one of those tragic occurrences which inevitably occur from time to time in human affairs."

Shortly afterward the jury returned a verdict of death by misadventure and they and the coroner expressed their sympathy with the parents and fiancé of the dead girl.

On the way home Colonel Doughty said to Ronald, "What on earth was that coroner fellow getting at by asking that question about Jane?"

"I suppose he was trying to find a possible reason for suicide."

"Why on earth should he do that?"

"Why indeed? But I suppose all those people feel they haven't done their job unless they ferret around."

"Well, I'm glad I put a stop to it."

They drove in silence for some time.

"Oh, why did you have to sit on the edge of a cliff?" suddenly said the colonel. "No, I'm sorry," he went on as suddenly. "I didn't mean to say that. But I keep on thinking of it. How it couldn't have happened if you'd both been somewhere else."

"I know," said Ronald. "So do I. Poor little Jane."

"Poor you," said Marion.

"Poor all of us," said Ronald. "Why did it have to happen?"

14

Mr. Plumb's Problem

TWO DAYS LATER MR. PLUMB READ A FULL ACCOUNT OF THE INQUEST. He actually arranged for a local paper to be sent to him so that he could read more than would appear in the national press. The report worried him very much. The picture painted to the coroner and the jury by Ronald and Jane's father was of the happiest possible relationship between her and Ronald. No one could possibly have told by reading a report of the inquest that not three months before the girl's death Ronald had consulted a solicitor with the object of finding some way to rid himself of the girl. Of course, it was possible that the man had had a change of heart. But it was not as though he were a young man. For a middle-aged man to want a court order against a girl to stop her from seeing him one day and to marry her the next was very odd. Not, of course, impossible but very odd. And then for the girl to die shortly afterward added oddity to oddity in a way which worried Mr. Plumb exceedingly. Like most lawyers he had a desire that the truth should be brought to light. It would have been quite easy for Ronald, having been told that it would be very difficult if not impossible to dispose of Jane by law, to dispose of her in fact. He could pretend to want to marry the girl, take her for a walk by the cliffside and, having made as sure as he could that no one was looking, push her over the side and run for help. Simple.

The thought that Ronald might be a murderer and that only he, Joseph Plumb, could supply a link in the chain of evidence to prove the murder, and that his lips were sealed, was terribly frustrating. But perhaps he was jumping too readily to conclusions. Perhaps the unfortunate man, so far from having murdered the girl, was overwhelmed with grief at a tragic accident.

Mr. Plumb began to find that he could not concentrate on his work. The conflicting thoughts battered at his mind. One moment Ronald was a guilty, unsuspected murderer, guilty of a most shocking crime. Killing a poor little girl of seventeen. The next moment he was a man who had suffered a dreadful blow through no fault of his own. At that moment Mr. Plumb almost felt that his own unworthy thoughts might be adding to Ronald's grief. Then back again would come the account at the inquest. If it was a pure accident, why didn't Ronald tell the whole story and explain that not long before he had wanted to be rid of the girl? Not the faintest suggestion of this was made. But perhaps he was being unjust. Why should an innocent man make public facts which might cause some suspicious-minded people—people perhaps like him, Joseph Plumb—to doubt his story? Assume all he said was correct. They were sitting ten yards from the edge. The girl walked to it, overbalanced or became dizzy and fell over. Why should the man say in those circumstances: 'I ought to tell you that not so long ago I wanted the girl out of my life.' Why ought he to say that if he was innocent? If that was right, his failure to mention the cause of his visit to a solicitor was equally consistent with guilt and innocence.

Mr. Plumb could not leave the matter alone. Night and day it obsessed him. At least *he* had to know. It might well be that he would not be entitled to go to the police, whatever he discovered. But he must find out. He could not go on as he was. His health and work would suffer. His clients too. In self-defense he must do something, and there was only one thing to do. He must talk to the man himself.

Once he had made this decision, Mr. Plumb picked up the

telephone. Then he put it down again. Ronald might refuse to see him if he asked for an appointment. Although that might at first seem suspicious in itself, it might simply be due to a grief-stricken man not wanting to be bothered with strangers. Why should he agree to see a solicitor who had advised him once? Mr. Plumb decided that he must call on Ronald without warning. If he was out, he would call again. And he would call again and again until he had seen him. He felt that, if only he could have a conversation with the man, he would know instinctively. It might be that, if he discovered guilt, he could do nothing about it. But at least the uncertainty would have gone. He remembered his friend's advice about telling his client to go to the police. That might well be wrong, as his friend had said. He would not tell the man to do anything, unless he were asked for moral advice. He would simply talk to him and try to find out.

The day after he had made up his mind, Mr. Plumb went to Eleanor Gardens. He did not go straight to Ronald's house. Rather like a guest who is too early for dinner, he walked slowly around the gardens, simply noting where the house was. Eventually he plucked up courage, went to No. 18 and rang. He noticed that his heart was beating loudly. It's ridiculous, he told himself. I'm a middle-aged solicitor calling on a one-time client to ask him a few questions. What's wrong with that? Why should I be frightened? I've nothing on my conscience. It's a free country. One man is entitled to call on another. Of course, the other is not bound to let him in. Well, that's a situation to be dealt with when it arises.

Meantime, for what seemed ages, the bell remained unanswered. Then Ronald opened the door. He did not at first recognize Mr. Plumb. He had only seen him once in his life. No doubt, if he'd seen him in the office where he'd seen him before, he would have recognized him, but out of that context his face meant nothing to Ronald, though, as he looked at it, he had a vague feeling of having seen it before.

"Yes?" he said inquiringly.

"My name is Plumb. I'm a solicitor. You consulted me a little time back."

"Oh, yes, of course. I'm so sorry. I haven't a good memory for faces."

"Might I have a word with you, Colonel Holbrook?"

"Certainly," said Ronald. "Please come in."

So the first hurdle was negotiated. He was to have his interview. Now what was he to say? Mr. Plumb's heart continued to beat loudly. Ronald led the way into the sitting room and invited Mr. Plumb to have a chair. Mr. Plumb sat down. There was complete silence. Ronald broke it.

"You wanted to see me about something?" he said.

"Yes," said Mr. Plumb, and then added, "I'm grateful to you for seeing me."

"Not at all," said Ronald.

Then there was silence again. Mr. Plumb had worried so much about getting an interview at all that he had not properly considered what to ask if he got the chance. You can't very well say to a man just like that: 'Did you by any chance murder your fiancée?' And, even if you did, it was easy enough for a man to say no, and to show him indignantly to the door. Nor was it easy for Mr. Plumb to pretend that he had come to offer sympathy when he knew perfectly well that that was not the object of the visit at all. Although, of course, he reflected, as he tried to argue out in his mind the difficulties, if I decide that he's innocent I should certainly offer my condolences then. I don't like subterfuges, but, in all the circumstances, couldn't I start like that? Meanwhile the silence continued, and soon it became a question not so much of what to say but how to say anything at all. Ronald eventually came to Mr. Plumb's rescue.

"What is it you wish to see me about?" he asked.

"I read the report of the inquest on Miss Doughty," said Mr. Plumb.

"Yes?" said Ronald.

"It must have been a great strain for you."

"Naturally," said Ronald, "but I assume that you haven't come here to tell me that."

"Not exactly," said Mr. Plumb.

He was finding it far more difficult than he had expected. He had so far gained no impression from Ronald at all. His calmness was equally consistent with guilt or innocence.

"It was a terrible thing to happen," said Mr. Plumb.

"Terrible," said Ronald.

Mr. Plumb suddenly decided he must take his foot off the brake.

"What troubles me," he said rather hurriedly, "is the fact that not three months ago you wanted to get rid of the girl and now she's got rid of. I'm afraid that's a very bald way of putting it."

"Not as bald as asking me if I pushed the girl over, Mr. Plumb. If that was what you wanted to find out, the answer is no."

"I see," said Mr. Plumb.

"That was it then?" asked Ronald.

"It was such an odd coincidence."

"It wasn't a coincidence at all," said Ronald. "I consulted you because at the time I felt that in view of my age it was wrong for me to let Jane get so attached to me."

"You put it rather differently when you saw me."

"No doubt you have the notes of what I said, but that was substantially the reason for my consulting you. Shortly afterward I came to the conclusion that things had gone too far for me to withdraw. I was deeply fond of Jane and so I asked her to marry me and she accepted. We should have been very happy. Now, is there anything more I can do for you? If it makes you feel any better, I should tell you that the coroner's officer also asked me—very politely, of course—if I'd murdered Jane. I gave him the same answer. The mere fact that I've said it twice doesn't make it any more the truth, but that's what it happens to be."

Ronald got up and Mr. Plumb was quite glad to do so too. He did not see how he could usefully carry the conversation further.

"I hope you'll forgive my calling on you," he said.

"I really don't know why you did," said Ronald, "but there's nothing to forgive. Good day."

Mr. Plumb walked away realizing that his visit had been a complete failure. Ronald had been too smooth perhaps, and this suggested guilt. But he did not know the man well at all. He may have been annoyed at his calling and his method of showing his annoyance may have been coolness. Some men bluster and shout when angered, others become icy cold. He had in fact walked into the house of a man whom he had met once and asked him if he was a murderer. A pretty cool thing to do. The man had answered no and shown him the door. What sign of guilt was that? He'd let his imagination run away with him.

But had he? Mr. Plumb then recalled his first interview and Ronald's great anxiety to stop the girl's advances. There must be some way, he had said. Well, there was. Kai Lung had said it. And how could there have been a happy engagement or marriage between a man and a girl when the girl had threatened the man in the way which Ronald had mentioned? Mr. Plumb could not reconcile the anxious Ronald on the first occasion with the cool Ronald on the second. And the picture of the girl was so different. The first was of a young but wicked woman. The second of a poor innocent girl falling to her death. But then, of course, there may be a reason for that. Once the girl's dead you don't start talking of her faults. They're soon forgotten. *De mortuis* and all that.

In other words, Mr. Plumb left Ronald in exactly the same state of uncertainty as he was in before the meeting. And now it was worse. Because he had seen the man to whom the truth was known. In the man's head lay the solution to his problem, and he had been unable to extract anything from it. But he must. Somehow or other he must. He was sorry now that he had had the interview so precipitately. He should have worked out a plan before seeing the man. But what could he do? There must be something. Almost Ronald's very words when he came to him for help.

15

The Letters

ABOUT A WEEK AFTER HIS INTERVIEW WITH MR. PLUMB, Ronald received an anonymous letter. It contained one word: "MURDERER." The word was cut out of some book or newspaper and pasted on the inside of a folding postcard. The address on the outside was in block capitals. He looked at it for some time and wondered what to do. Go straight to the police? They could do nothing on that evidence. Go to Jane's parents? What was the point? And why put ideas—however farfetched they might think them—into other people's heads? Ronald felt sure that no one in Eleanor Gardens, with the possible exception of Mr. Sinclair, felt anything but pity for him. But rumors spread so quickly and so easily, particularly if they are unpleasant. The Doughtys might easily mention the matter to other people. Might not some people say to themselves: "Good gracious, I never thought of that. I don't suppose there's anything in it. I wonder."

He was settling down again in Eleanor Gardens. Everyone treated him as they had before Jane's death, only they were even more kindly. Except, of course, Mr. Sinclair, whom he hardly ever spoke to anyway. He didn't want people to start eying him strangely or stopping their conversation suddenly if he came on them unawares. People were strange. Even friends could start wondering. Once the poisoned word is mentioned, it floats through the air, into people's ears, into their minds and then out of their mouths.

So he decided to say nothing about it for the moment. He could always say later that he had a clear conscience and treated the matter with contempt. But he did wonder who had sent the letter. It couldn't be Mr. Plumb. A respectable solicitor couldn't possibly do a thing like that. Ronald was, of course, aware that Mr. Plumb must have considered how the tragedy occurred and been worried by his knowledge of the case, but he was quite unaware of the extent to which the matter was preying on Mr. Plumb's mind. If he had known that, he might not have dismissed so easily the possibility of his being the sender of the letter. Had he known that, he might have suspected Mr. Plumb not of feeling sure that Ronald was a murderer but of wanting to make him go to the police and so get some further investigation into the matter. Not a method which a solicitor in his right mind would dream of adopting, but just conceivably something which a man, whatever his calling, might be driven to do by his gnawing doubts, doubts which temporarily deprived him of the power of clear or right thinking.

Well, if it wasn't Mr. Plumb, and Ronald felt sure that it was not, who was it? Mr. Sinclair? He had certainly behaved very oddly when he came allegedly to condole. He asked very odd questions for a comforter, even for one who was not a personal friend. Indeed, questions which came very oddly from a stranger. If Ronald hadn't stopped him, it looked almost as though he had put him in the witness box and was cross-examining him. Mr. Sinclair, too, was an odd person. No one knew much about him. He was always perfectly polite and had never sought to annoy any of his neighbors, but he might be one of those queer individuals who are not absolutely normal. Then Ronald remembered that Mr. Sinclair had always smiled very pleasantly at Jane, though his greetings to other neighbors were usually more distant. Perhaps he loved the child and was so distraught by her death that he had to do something about it. It wasn't very likely but he was certainly a possibility.

Who else could there be? Surely not Mrs. Vintage. She certainly was very monosyllabic but she was always very friendly and not the sort of person to wage a vendetta against anyone. Of course, she was old and old people did go a bit mad, but after the way she had spoken to him both before and after the inquest, he couldn't think that Mrs. Vintage could possibly have sent such a letter. The two barristers he ruled out at once. Even if they had suspicions of him—and he felt sure they hadn't—they wouldn't dream of behaving in such a manner. If it were found out, they would be ruined professionally. So would Mr. Plumb. The only difference between them and Mr. Plumb was that he had knowledge which they did not share. Mr. Plumb knew that, when he had gone to him for advice, he very much wanted to be as far away from Jane as possible.

Could it be Mr. Highcastle? Could he have become so angry at losing a possible commission that, when he read the report of the inquest, he thought he would get his own back. Most unlikely. Businessmen want to make money, not to get involved in personal disputes. Who else? Melrose, the practical joker, was undoubtedly a malicious person in one sense. He enjoyed discomfiting people. But he wasn't in any way vicious. He would cheerfully make a man look a fool or create an embarrassing situation, but the end product of his behavior was always something to laugh at—for someone at any rate, if not the actual victim. There was nothing whatever to laugh at in the postcard for anyone. It couldn't possibly be he.

He thought of all his other neighbors, and dismissed them one by one, in each case with certainty. In the end he was left only with Mr. Sinclair, a possibility, and Mr. Plumb, a most unlikely suggestion. Indeed, he only returned to him for lack of anyone else to suspect. Had it been possible to see another person's mind, Mr. Plumb might have become Suspect No. 1, because it was in a horribly disturbed condition.

Having decided to do nothing about the matter, Ronald went about his affairs as normally as possible. He did look more closely than usual at Mr. Sinclair when they met in the street, and he fancied that Mr. Sinclair looked more closely at him. On one occasion indeed Mr. Sinclair half stopped as though he were going to speak to him, but then he went on again, just saying, as he normally did, "Good day to you."

A week later another letter came. This was rather more menacing. Again it was a folding postcard and again the words were printed and pasted on it. They were: "I SAW YOU."

This was frightening. By itself it meant nothing, but coupled with the other postcard it read: "Murderer, I saw you." In other words, the sender was saying that he had seen Ronald push Jane off the cliff. And the serious thing from Ronald's point of view was this: What was to prevent someone from coming along and saying that he had seen Ronald push Jane over the cliff? The man might have been in London at the time, but what was to prevent him from saying that he was on the cliff, out of sight lying down? He would have to explain why he did not go straight to the police or come forward at the inquest. But there could be explanations for such behavior. Such as a dislike of helping the police or something of that kind. The sender was probably of bad character. And this thought prompted in Ronald's mind the most probable explanation of the man's behavior. He was preparing the ground for blackmail.

What was he to do now? Go straight to the police? Probably that was the best course, but it would mean that in the end one way or another it would become known that someone had said that he or she had seen Ronald commit murder. Well, most people wouldn't believe it but it would undoubtedly start rumors flying and affect his position in the neighborhood.

Now he had to consider again who might have done it. This was surely someone other than Mr. Sinclair or Mr. Plumb, unless both had gone mad. But perhaps Mr. Sinclair was mad already. Why had he nearly stopped and spoken to him? He had never done so before. Ronald felt that he had better call on Mr. Sinclair and see if he could find out anything. Then another idea occurred to him. Why not go and see Mr. Plumb and consult him? He felt he needed advice. If he went to another solicitor, there would be two people who knew part of the story. It was true that a solicitor was not supposed to give away clients' confidences, but how could one be sure that he didn't tell his wife or a colleague? Or he might have clerks who would learn of the matter. Much better to have one man only in his confidence. And he could advise him about going to the police. He could even go with him if necessary. But that probably wasn't a very good idea. From what he had read

in the papers, it usually seemed to be men who were giving themselves up who went to the police with their solicitors.

And there was another advantage in going to see Mr. Plumb. If,
against all the probabilities, Mr. Plumb was the sender of the letters, Ronald might be able to sense this from his reaction when
confronted with them. Yes, he must see Mr. Plumb. Of course, it
would mean that Mr. Plumb, who was the only person who knew
of his one-time anxiety to get away from Jane, would now know of
the anonymous allegations. But Plumb couldn't tell anyone about
them, and the fact that Ronald brought the letters along of his own
accord might resolve in his favor any doubts which the solicitor
might still have. Mr. Plumb would surely think that, if he were a
murderer, he would not be so foolish as to add to the evidence in
his solicitor's possession.

Having decided to see Mr. Plumb, Ronald considered whether
to call on Mr. Sinclair first. Eventually he thought it was a good
idea, particularly because he could tell the result to Mr. Plumb.

The same morning he called on Mr. Sinclair, who appeared surprised to see him.

"Mr. Sinclair," said Ronald, after he had been invited in, "the
other day you nearly stopped me in the street. As you have never
done that before, would you mind telling me what you nearly said
to me?"

"I thought it might hurt your feelings, so I passed on."

"Would you mind saying it to me now?"

"It would still hurt your feelings."

"All the same, I would risk that. I should very much like to
know what it was."

"If you insist, I will tell you," said Mr. Sinclair, "but you mustn't
complain if you think I shouldn't say it. After all, I only *nearly*
said it."

"I won't complain."

"I was going to ask you how much you missed Jane—Miss
Doughty."

"What an extraordinary question."

"I know. That is why I did not ask it."

"But I can't think why you wanted to ask it."

"Because I can't get the pair of you out of my mind. Since I heard of the dreadful tragedy, I keep on putting myself in your position. I sit on the cliff and watch her go to the edge. And then I get nearer to the edge. And then sometimes I have her and sometimes I don't. And once I pushed her. Don't ask me to explain why. I suppose it may have been to get rid of the agony. As long as she was standing there on the edge I had the terrible fear that she might fall. I suppose I knew that, as soon as she fell, that fear would go. It would be replaced by grief. Which is the worse, an agony of fear or the deepest grief? I felt I wanted to know how you felt, so that I could tell how I should feel. I don't know if you follow me."

"Are you suggesting that I pushed Jane over?"

"Heavens, no," said Mr. Sinclair. "You weren't near her. You couldn't reach from ten yards away. Quite impossible. You were a full ten yards away, weren't you?"

"Yes, I was," said Ronald, "but why do you continually think about it?"

"Don't you?" said Mr. Sinclair.

Ronald did not answer.

"Consciously or unconsciously," said Mr. Sinclair, "I am going through all your emotions, thinking all your thoughts or what my brain tells me must be your emotions and thoughts."

"Why?"

"I can't tell you. I feel impelled to do so. Perhaps it's because of the nearness of the tragedy. You live almost opposite, and Jane too. I saw you every week. Sometimes every day in the week. I can see and touch a person who has been through this overwhelming experience. You are so near to me that sometimes I feel almost that I am you."

"Did you ever feel like writing to me, Mr. Sinclair?" asked Ronald.

"Several times," said Mr. Sinclair. "I got as far as starting a letter but I tore it up."

"So you never did write?"

"No."

"Do you think perhaps that you yourself have been undergoing such a strain that you did write to me and have forgotten?"

"That's impossible. My memory isn't all that good, but it's not six weeks since the inquest and I couldn't fail to remember posting a letter or dropping it into your box."

"The mind does queer things sometimes," said Ronald.

"You don't have to tell me that," said Mr. Sinclair. "Mine is playing havoc with me now."

He paused momentarily and then went on quickly, "Why didn't you save her?"

Ronald simply looked at him.

"I'm sorry," said Mr. Sinclair. "You shouldn't have asked me those questions. It's such a relief to answer them. Now that you know how I feel, it somehow helps."

"You hardly knew Jane. I can't understand why you should be so upset."

"Nor can I. She was a sweet little girl. I enjoyed watching her, but I've never exchanged more than a few words with her. I suppose when the accident happened I thought to myself, 'How awful if it had been me.' And from that moment something in my brain took command and tried to tell me that it was me. Do you keep on thinking: 'Why wasn't I nearer, why didn't I save her?' Do you wriggle toward the edge in your thoughts and put out a hand to save her?"

"I'm sorry you're so upset, Mr. Sinclair, but I don't think that my thoughts are your business."

"Indeed, no. I'm sorry. I couldn't resist asking."

"Are you sure you resisted writing, Mr. Sinclair?" asked Ronald, and looked him full in the face. Mr. Sinclair did not return his gaze but looked away quickly.

"Yes, I'm sure," said Mr. Sinclair. "But why do you ask? Have you had a letter from me?"

"How could I, if you've never written?"

"Perhaps it wasn't signed and you wondered if it was me. But then the address would have told you. Unless it was on blank paper and someone had forgotten to put the address."

Ronald thought quickly. Should he produce the letters and see the reaction? On the whole he decided not to do so. Mr. Sinclair would presumably deny responsibility, and he would then have disclosed the existence of the letters to someone in Eleanor Gardens. Although Mr. Sinclair did not speak much to people, on a matter where, whatever the truth was, he felt strongly, he might mention it. Once mentioned, it would go round the neighborhood with lightning speed.

"I just wondered," said Ronald. "If you tell me you've never written, I must accept it."

"But something must have made you ask."

"Of course," said Ronald. "But, as you've answered the question, there's no point in going into the matter. Thank you very much for seeing me."

Ronald left Mr. Sinclair and went home to make an appointment with Mr. Plumb. But the visit to Mr. Sinclair had certainly shown that he might have been responsible for the letters. It is true that a normal person, who had sent the letters, would not have said all that Mr. Sinclair had said. But, on any view of the matter, Mr. Sinclair was not normal. He was certainly a fair suspect. After all, who else could it be? He was sure now that it would not be Mr. Plumb. The coincidence that both Plumb and Sinclair were somewhat round the bend would be too great. It still might be someone completely different. A professional blackmailer who read the papers. But, he thought, a professional would surely want some evidence, some real evidence, against a man before he struck. Otherwise the police would almost certainly be called in and he would eventually be trapped. And no one but Mr. Plumb knew that he had tried to get away from Jane. Mr. Sinclair certainly did not know. Nor, whatever else he was, was he a professional blackmailer. His was a mysterious calling perhaps, but it was in the highest degree unlikely that he had for years been carrying on the business of blackmail from the same address without being found out.

16

Mr. Plumb's Relief

MR. PLUMB WAS SURPRISED when Ronald asked for an appointment. He was also to some extent relieved that he might be able to get to grips with the matter again. He postponed two other appointments and saw Ronald the same afternoon.

"What do you make of these, Mr. Plumb?" asked Ronald, and watched the solicitor carefully as he looked at them.

"Have you any idea who may have sent them?" asked Mr. Plumb.

"I know of one possibility," said Ronald, and explained about Mr. Sinclair.

"It sounds probable," said Mr. Plumb. "People with unhinged minds do that sort of thing."

"What am I to do? Go to the police?"

"Yes, I think so," said Mr. Plumb, "but it wants consideration." He thought for a little, and then went on: "Before I advise you, Colonel Holbrook," he said, "I must in your own interest go further into your own position."

"I thought you'd done so when you came to see me."

"That wasn't a professional interview. I was not then advising you."

"I suppose you came for your own peace of mind," said Ronald.

Mr. Plumb looked at him sharply before answering. Then, "Yes, I suppose you can call it that."

"Well, I hope you were satisfied."

"As you ask the question, Colonel, I must tell you that I was not. But that may be my fault. To be quite frank, I still have difficulty in reconciling your sudden change of front. When you saw me first you were desperate. At that time there appeared to be no definite way out of your difficulties. I'm sure that at our interview neither of us imagined that the solution would be in the girl's death. But that death could not have been brought about if you had not—apparently—changed your mind and offered to marry the girl. I must admit that that worried me from my own point of view as a spectator. I must speak frankly to you. What went on in my mind was this: Was I the only witness of a murder and was I nevertheless unable to do anything about it? I once read a story about a woman who saw her son-in-law kill her daughter but the shock paralyzed her and made her dumb so that she was unable to communicate her knowledge to the police. The sense of frustration must have been appalling. I was not in as bad a position as that because I certainly could not be sure that it was murder. But, if it was not, it was a very tragic coincidence."

"Why are you telling me all this?"

"Because, in my view, you have a right to know what is in the mind of your solicitor, so that you can consult someone else if you prefer it. The reason I say that you have a right to know my mind is because with this knowledge you may think I am too biased against you and that my advice may be biased accordingly."

"What is your advice?" asked Ronald.

"Normally, if a person receives letters like this, the proper course is to go at once to the police. Whether the letters are a preliminary to blackmail or the outward expression of a lunatic mind, they are criminally libelous of you. Therefore, normally one would automatically go to the police."

"You say 'normally,'" said Ronald.

"This is not a normal case. Please don't get annoyed at what I am about to say, but it's necessary for me to say it. Suppose, in fact, you did kill the girl. The less you see of the police from your point of view the better."

"Why?"

"Because in conversation with them they may elicit from you the facts which I know. Naturally I shouldn't tell them myself. But it might become extremely embarrassing for you and for me if they asked you questions which you answered untruthfully to my knowledge. I should then have to withdraw from the case. And that very fact would naturally make the police suspect you. On the other hand, if you told the truth, that is, told them what you originally told me, they might suspect you even more. And then they would try hard to find the writer of the letters, not so much to protect you as to find evidence against you. And, in my opinion, if they found someone who says he saw you push the girl over, there would be strong evidence against you of murder."

"But no one can say they saw me push her if I didn't."

"You forget two things, Colonel Holbrook. First, that what I am saying is on the assumption that you *did* kill the girl. Secondly, that whether you did or did not, someone might say that he had seen you push her over, either because he imagined it or because for reasons of his own—blackmail, madness or something else—he chooses to lie about you."

"Are you telling me that, whether I am innocent or guilty—and I can assure you I'm innocent—if I go to the police I may be suspected of murder and even charged with it?"

"That is so, if somehow or other they learn that you were desperately anxious to get away from the girl not three months before she died."

"Isn't there something wrong with the law then? Here I am, a perfectly innocent person, and I may have to stand my trial for murder? And when I'm acquitted—as I'm bound to be—there'll always be people who will suspect me. It doesn't seem fair to me."

"It certainly isn't fair, if you're innocent, Colonel Holbrook, but is it the law's fault? There may be many improvements which could usefully be made to the law, but a person who is plagued by coincidence will always be suspect under any form of law. Usually they are not coincidences and the person is guilty. Usually when a man wants a girl out of the way and shortly afterward she falls over a cliff in his presence it isn't a coincidence. She was pushed over. But where it is a coincidence you must surely blame Providence, not the law. The law has to take things as it finds them. If the law sees a man with a smoking revolver standing over the body of someone against whom he's sworn vengeance, isn't the law bound to say that it looks as if the man was guilty? It may be that, when the facts are investigated, it is possible that he had taken the revolver from the hands of the real murderer, who made his escape, and that the threats of vengeance were due to momentary anger and that the man in question was a great friend of the dead man; but you must admit that, until these facts come to light, the strong probability is that the man standing over the body was the murderer."

"Well, I can't throw the blame on anyone else. I was the only person there."

"How d'you know?" asked Mr. Plumb. "What about the sender of the letters?"

"D'you think there really was someone there?"

"I've no idea," said Mr. Plumb, "but there could have been."

"Then, if he saw me push the girl, why didn't he go to the police?"

"You must remember, Colonel Holbrook, that he didn't see you push her because you didn't push her."

"Then why didn't he go to the police and say I didn't push her?"

"Well, no one said you did and the person may not have wanted to be involved in giving evidence."

"Then what is he or she after now?"

"Possibly it's your Mr. Sinclair who is merely relieving himself at your expense. Or someone else like that. Possibly it's a preliminary to blackmail."

"But, surely, Mr. Plumb, a blackmailer to have any reasonable chance of success must have some concrete evidence—a letter or something or an independent witness."

"I suppose so, usually," said Mr. Plumb.

"As we are speaking frankly," said Ronald, "who can you think of who has any special information about me except yourself?"

"Are you suggesting that I sent those letters, sir?"

"You have told me that you suspected me of murder. I can't say that I really suspected you of sending the letters, but I couldn't think of anyone else to fill the bill except you, until I interviewed Sinclair."

"Are you now satisfied, sir?" said Mr. Plumb with some asperity.

"Really, Mr. Plumb, murder is at least on a par with blackmail. It's no better, shall we say. You make no bones about suspecting me of murder. I really don't know why you should be so indignant at the possibility of my suspecting you of blackmail."

"I am a solicitor, sir."

"Meaning, I suppose, that that makes you respectable. Well, so am I respectable, Mr. Plumb. You say to me that, if I'm not a murderer, there's been a horrible coincidence. Why can't I similarly say to you that, if you're not a blackmailer, there's been another coincidence, that you're the only person I can think of who has information about me which, according to you, might be dangerous for me to have disclosed? If *I* can take your accusation calmly—"

"It was not an accusation, sir."

"Nor was mine. Nor is it. But when I received letters of that kind I naturally tried to think of everyone I knew who might conceivably have sent them. Not only had I given certain information to you, but you actually called at my house uninvited and with no appointment. That was a pretty odd thing for a solicitor to do, Mr. Plumb. Have you ever done it before?"

"I can't say that I have."

Mr. Plumb was now slightly on the defensive. Moreover, he recollected the tussle that went on in his mind before he called on Ronald. So he dropped the "sir" of indignation. Ronald noticed this and smiled slightly.

"Aren't honors about even, Mr. Plumb?" he asked in a friendly way.

"Well," said Mr. Plumb, "if you put it like that, perhaps I was a bit hasty. But I'd be struck off the Rolls, you know, if I did anything like that, apart from any other punishment."

"And very properly," said Ronald. "And I would be sent to

prison for life. So shall we drop the personalities and go on to consider what I should do?"

"Very well," said Mr. Plumb.

"One of the difficulties is that I do not want anything in the nature of a scandal in my neighborhood. I have lived there many years and want to go on doing so. But any form of court proceedings would be very unsatisfactory from my point of view. If I go to the police there are likely to be proceedings, aren't there?"

"If they catch the man, certainly."

"That's just what I don't want."

"What is it you do want?"

"To be protected from getting letters like this, of course."

"Well, how can you be protected without getting the police to protect you? I suppose you might hire a detective agency to investigate the matter, but they're not very satisfactory, and very expensive."

"What do you advise?"

Mr. Plumb thought for a short time.

"I presume that you want me to advise you on the basis that you're an entirely innocent man."

"Of course."

"You will understand that, if you told me you were guilty, my advice might be different."

"I've told you several times that there is no question of that."

"You mustn't be impatient with me, Colonel Holbrook. Suppose I advise you on the basis that you're innocent but you are in fact guilty. By following my advice you could get yourself convicted. And then you might feel that your lawyer had let you down. 'Why did you tell me to do that?' you might say or at least think. 'Why didn't you tell me not to do the other?' And so on. I'm not concerned with my responsibility. That's simple enough. You tell me you're innocent. It's not my business to disbelieve you, and advise you as if you were guilty. But I do think that I have a duty to warn you that, if in fact you're guilty, my advice may be very bad advice from your point of view."

"So you have said and I understand you," said Ronald. "I take it then that, if you advise me on the assumption that I'm innocent, and I am in fact innocent, I shall come to no harm."

"No harm with the law certainly," said Mr. Plumb. "I do not believe that any respectable man who is innocent will be convicted of a serious crime. Unless possibly there's a conspiracy against him. That couldn't be the case here, could it?"

"I'm not sure," said Ronald. "You say no harm with the law. What other harm can I come to?"

"You've mentioned that yourself. If you go to the police, I cannot guarantee that there will not be proceedings, and, if there were, there would be publicity. That simply cannot be avoided."

"Supposing I had told you I was guilty—what would your advice have been?"

"Then," said Mr. Plumb, "I should have told you that it was your moral duty to go to the police and confess your crime."

"I shouldn't have needed a solicitor to tell me that."

"But a solicitor has some duty to the public and, if a murderer consults him, it is in my view necessary for him to remind his client of his moral duty. If you refused to accept that advice, I should advise you to make no statements to the police and not to get involved with them if you could help it."

"And the letters?"

"Grin and bear them."

"And if they were followed by demands for money?"

"Refuse to pay and do nothing."

"And if the blackmailer went to the police about me?"

"Do nothing and say nothing, except that you would consult your legal advisers and then leave the matter to me."

"And what would you do?"

"Tell the police that you would not make a statement."

"That would make them think I was guilty," said Ronald.

"Of course it would," said Mr. Plumb, "but they would still have to prove you guilty. And if there were no actual witnesses of the murder who could satisfactorily account for not coming forward before, I don't see how your guilt could be proved without your assistance. And that assistance I would advise you, as your lawyer, not your spiritual adviser, not to give. I don't see how the police could get a conviction without proof of a motive, and I am the only person who knows of that. And, of course, they would get nothing from me."

"I forgot to mention that there is a house agent who knows I wanted to leave."

"You'd put your house in his hands for sale?"

"Yes."

"Had you told him why?"

"Certainly not, but I had said that it was urgent."

"So they'd be able to prove that you wanted to leave the neighborhood. That would be something. Your difficulty would be this: The police might be able to call one or more unsatisfactory witnesses to say you pushed the girl over. They could be very severely cross-examined and would be of little value if you were able to go into the witness box and deny your guilt. But you wouldn't be able to do that."

"Why not?"

"Because your counsel and I wouldn't let you. It would be our duty to defend you, even though we knew you were guilty, but not by putting up a false case. All we could do would be to submit that the prosecution's case hadn't been proved. But just a moment. Let me think."

Mr. Plumb thought. "I'm not even sure, now that I come to think of it," he said, "that we could cross-examine the witnesses about their not coming forward before, because we would know their evidence was true."

"Even if it was true, and I assure you it wasn't in fact, they may have been inventing it. They may not have been there at all."

"Yes," said Mr. Plumb. "I suppose that, if that was a possibility, we should be entitled to submit that they were liars and had seen nothing, and for that purpose to cross-examine them to show they weren't there."

"But why couldn't I go into the witness box and deny everything if that would get me off?"

"Because we would know you were guilty and would refuse to appear for you if you insisted on doing it."

"So that, if there were a death penalty, you might insist on your client being hanged?"

"In a sense, yes. And why not? There are all sorts of lies a solicitor might suggest to get his client off, but we don't do that in this country."

"So it would be better for me to defend myself."

"If you were prepared to commit perjury, certainly."

"And no one but you and my counsel would know the truth?"

"Presumably not."

"And you would do nothing about it?"

"We couldn't."

"I find this fascinating," said Ronald. "That's why I've asked you so much. But I must assure you yet again that the problem does not arise in this case. I not only tell you I am innocent, but I am."

"Very well," said Mr. Plumb, "we will proceed on that assumption."

"Even being innocent," said Ronald, "would it be a sensible thing for me to tell the police what you know from my first interview with you?"

"That's a very difficult question. It is usually sensible for an innocent man to tell the police everything, but, when it isn't essential to do so and when the failure to tell them does not amount to a lie, there may be cases where it's not advisable to volunteer a statement about something which they don't know. This may be such a case. But the danger there is that, if that matter comes out later, the failure to disclose it before might look like a sign of a guilty conscience."

"Well, what do you advise?"

"On the whole," said Mr. Plumb, "in view of your anxiety to avoid publicity, I should do nothing at this stage. If the sender was Mr. Sinclair, you may have frightened him by your questions and nothing more may happen. If it was a lunatic or a criminal, he might by luck be put under restraint before he could do any more. So I should wait and see what happens. You can always telephone me or come and see me. But, if you weren't so anxious about publicity, I should say 'Go to the police at once.' "

"Thank you, Mr. Plumb. I'm grateful to you for going into the matter so fully," said Ronald, and got up to go.

When he had left, Mr. Plumb felt quite all right again. He no longer had to wonder about the case. The man was his client and, guilty or innocent, he must do the best he could for him. It was being out of the case which had worried him so much. Once he was in it, it didn't matter. If he was helping a guilty man to avoid the consequences of his crime, he was only doing so by proper methods and it was his duty to have done what he did. If the man was innocent, so much the better. He was no longer frustrated and slept better that night than he had done for a long time.

17

The Agent

WHEN RONALD ARRIVED HOME there was a letter for him. It had been sent by hand. It was like the others and read: "I REALLY DID."

His first reaction was to telephone Mr. Plumb. But he had probably left the office by then, and Ronald was rather glad. It gave him more time to think. The receipt of a third letter did not seem to carry the matter any further. If nothing more happened than that, he could simply throw the letters away or keep them in a file and ignore the whole thing. The question was whether someone was going to appear, and, if so, who.

This question was answered the same evening when Ronald went to the door to answer the bell. A stranger was there, a man who looked about fifty-five, not shabbily dressed but wearing a suit that he or possibly someone else had worn for some years.

"Forgive me calling," he said in a voice which had originally been cockney but which now had a heavy veneer of cultured accent over it. "You will think this very strange. My calling at all, I mean. I nearly didn't but then I felt I should. I was here this morning actually and I almost came in then, but then I thought it might be presumptuous. So I went away again. And then later I thought, 'Well, perhaps I should. One never knows.' So here I am. Please forgive the intrusion."

"If you'd tell me what you're calling about," said Ronald, "I might learn whether there was anything to forgive."

"Of course, of course," said the man. "But it may be absolutely nothing. Then there will be something to forgive, won't there, and I hope you will. I think I would if it happened to me. But then, of course, one can't really put oneself into other people's shoes. Because no two minds are alike. Shoes can be, of course."

"Would you come to the point?" said Ronald.

"I'm a bit embarrassed, as a matter of fact, because you'll very likely say that I'm just an interfering busybody and I shouldn't like you to think that. Perhaps it is a bit interfering. All the same, I felt I should."

"Should what?" asked Ronald.

"Call on you. It's a piece of impertinence really and I'll quite understand if you just ask me to go. That's why I didn't come in this morning. He'll just tell me to buzz off, I said to myself. And then, when I was thinking about it this evening, I thought, 'No, I ought to go. If there's nothing in it, it can't do any harm. After all, it's I who'll have wasted a journey.' It's not as though I'd asked you to call on me. That would have been a bit hot. But it was the way he moved. Furtive, you might say. So I thought I should."

"The way who moved?"

"The man I was telling you about. Yes, furtive, that's the word."

"What man?"

"He was there one minute and gone the next. Forgive me if I'm a bit incoherent. But actually I'm a bit nervous at having come at all. I'm embarrassed. That's the word, embarrassed."

"Who was this man and what did he want?"

"D'you think I could come in? I feel awkward standing on the doorstep like this. Besides, if it's anything at all, it might be confidential and we don't want to tell all the neighbors, do we? But there I go. I don't suppose there's anything in it. Just a circular, I expect."

"Come in," said Ronald, and took the stranger into the sitting room and offered him a chair.

"That's very civil of you," said the man, "but I'd prefer to stand. I'll twiddle my thumbs if I sit down. I always do when I'm embarrassed. But you can't twiddle them standing up very well. But when you sit down you put them in your lap and then—"

"Please, Mr. . . . Mr. . . ."

"You'd like to know my name? Good. That shows you can't be too angry. It's Hatchett, as a matter of fact. Not very like one, am I? But there it is."

"Will you please tell me what you saw this morning?"

"That's why I'm here. Did you have a circular put in your letter box this morning?"

"No," said Ronald.

"No? Oh, good. Then my instinct may have been right. It wasn't just a circular. Unless, of course, you don't take any notice of them and throw them away without thinking. Then you might not remember."

"Did you see someone put a letter in my box this morning?"

"Oh, I *am* relieved," said Mr. Hatchett. "My instinct *was* right. You did have something unusual. It was the way he moved."

"Could you recognize him again?" asked Ronald.

"Oh, yes, I had a good look at him. Then you're pleased I came? You don't want to throw me out?"

"No. I'm grateful to you for coming."

Mr. Hatchett's manner suddenly changed. "Oh, I am glad, sir," he said, but he was no longer twittering. "Now I can put my cards on the table. I'm afraid I was behaving rather oddly. That was just in case I was wrong. I'll tell you what happened. I'm an inquiry agent, as a matter of fact, and I was coming along here this morning when I saw a man acting, as the police would say, suspiciously. First of all he walked right around the square, but all the time he was looking in the direction of your house. When he was about twenty yards away from it, he felt in his pocket and brought out what looked like a letter. I should tell you that, as a matter of what you might call automatic action, when I saw him walking around the square in what struck me as a rather odd manner, I concealed myself as well as I could behind the pillar of that end house and I'm sure he didn't notice me. When he reached your house he looked all around him, then darted to the letter box, put something in, darted away again and then sauntered off as though nothing had happened. Now, any ordinary person who'd seen it would have wondered what it was all about. But it was unlikely that any ordinary person would have seen it, as he tried to make sure of that before he dropped the letter in. But as an inquiry agent of many years' experience I realized that something pretty odd was going on. Of course, I couldn't be sure, so I hope you'll forgive what I may call my verbal disguise."

"What did you think the man was doing?"

"Well, sir, I'll hazard a guess. You're being blackmailed. That was a ransom note or whatever you like to call it."

"It wasn't," said Ronald.

"Well, I'm surprised," said Mr. Hatchett. "Nothing of the sort?"

"It may have been something of the sort."

"Ah, I thought so. Well, sir, can I do anything for you? I'll be quite frank with you, sir. When I saw this chap drop the note in, I thought there might be some business in it for me. In most of these cases people don't like going to the police and, to be perfectly truthful, purely for my own advantage I decided to pay you a call. If you don't want my services, sir, there's no harm done and I'll be off. But we inquiry agents don't always get our business in the normal way. And I certainly don't wait at home for the telephone to ring or someone to call. I go out to get the business. It's surprising what you can pick up. Quite a lot of it in pubs. And I keep my eyes and ears open. This time it was my eyes. If you don't want to hire me, that's quite all right, sir. I'll leave my name and address and later on if you or the police want me to identify the chap, I'll do so with pleasure. On the other hand, if I can help you—and, I'll be frank, myself at the same time—here I am at your service."

"What actually could you do?" asked Ronald.

"Well, for one thing I could pick up the chap for you. I know the type. He'll be here again."

"Why should he come again? Why shouldn't he use the ordinary mail? Then he couldn't be traced."

"Couldn't he, sir? How does he know you haven't gone to the police already? Postmarks can tell you a lot sometimes. There've been quite a number of cases where blackmailers or poison-pen writers have been picked up at a mailbox."

"But if he lives in one part of London, he can post it from another."

"He may think he's being followed."

"Then why isn't he frightened of coming here? If I'd gone to the police, people might be watching this house all the time. From other houses, I mean. He couldn't tell he was under observation."

"Well, you may be right, sir. But the ways of these birds are many and various. And I just think he'll be here again."

"And suppose he does come again?"

"We can ask him in to have a chat."

"And if he refused?"

"We could call the police."

"What would they do?"

"Well, of course, that depends on what's in the notes."

"What would you charge to keep a lookout for him?"

"Well, sir, that all depends on how long it takes. We charge by the day."

"How much?"

"Ten guineas for the first day or part of a day, and five guineas for every day or part of a day thereafter. That's for day work only. If you want a round-the-clock watch, that's much more expensive. It takes three men. That'd be twenty-five guineas for the first day and fifteen thereafter."

"It's very expensive."

"Depends how you look at it, sir. It is a lot, I agree. But what's it going to cost not to employ me? You've got to think of that."

"At the moment it costs nothing."

"Good, sir. Then I've come at the right moment. These devils will squeeze the life out of you, unless you go to the police at once. I gather you don't want to do that, sir."

"I don't know," said Ronald. "I might."

"Well, sir, if I may give you a bit of advice free, you go to the police. It's far the best course. I know I'm speaking against my own interest, but quite frankly they'll be of far more use to you than I can. They can arrest people or get them to come to the station for questioning. And, if it comes to a court case, they'll always let you call yourself Mr. X. Really, sir, if there's no particular reason why you don't want to go to the police, I should give up the idea of employing me and go straight to the nearest station. No ten guineas a day then. All free, gratis and for nothing. And, after all, you're a taxpayer. Might as well have something for your money."

"I have several times known the identity of a Mr. X. Indeed, occasionally it's been talked about quite freely and even published in the foreign press."

"True enough, sir, but isn't that mostly in important cases? Dukes or millionaires, or that sort of thing. You'd probably get away with it quite easily. It's of course just possible that somehow or other one or two of your immediate neighbors might learn about it. But no doubt they're good friends and you can then explain it all. I don't suppose it's so bad anyway. If you'll forgive my hazarding a guess, it was some indiscretion, I expect, sir. It's not as though you'd committed murder."

"No," said Ronald, "I haven't. But I must think. Forgive me."

"Of course, sir. Take your time."

It was an odd coincidence, thought Ronald, that an inquiry agent happened to be in Eleanor Gardens just at the time that the anonymous letter-writer was there. Was it a coincidence? Or was this the man himself and was he going to pretend to watch for someone else who didn't exist? Was that the object of the notes—to get him to pay large fees? This was quite possible. What should he do? Go straight to the police or trap the man himself first? Who was the man? What made him think that the letters would worry Ronald? What could he know beyond what he had read in the papers?

Ronald eventually decided to employ the man for a day or two but to keep a watch on him. He could always go to the police when he wanted, and, if Hatchett was fraudulent and was himself the writer of the notes, it might be useful if he could prove this against him. Hatchett would then have been guilty of obtaining money by false pretenses, which would give Ronald some hold over him.

"I'm not a rich man," said Ronald eventually, "but I'm prepared to employ you for a day or two to try and find this man."

"Thank you, sir. May I know what is in the notes?"

"That isn't necessary at present," said Ronald. "All I want you to do in the first instance is to find this man."

"Very good, sir. Shall I get in touch with the police myself? I often work in close touch with them."

"That won't be necessary at first," said Ronald.

"Very good, sir. Do you want an all-round-the-clock watch? Personally I don't think that's necessary."

"I think a day watch will be enough at first. Could you start now?"

"Certainly, sir. I usually ask for the first half of the first day's fee in advance, sir, but, as you don't know me and I might never appear again, I'll waive that. But if you could see your way to pay me at the end of each day, I'd be grateful."

"Certainly," said Ronald.

For some days Mr. Hatchett was on watch but no more letters arrived.

"Perhaps he won't come any more," said Ronald as he paid him his fee. "I have your telephone number. I'll ring if I want you again."

"Thank you, sir. I shall be at your service. But don't forget, sir, the police station is only a quarter of a mile away. Far less expensive than me."

A few days later another letter was delivered by hand. "WHAT ARE YOU GOING TO DO ABOUT IT?" it said.

Ronald telephoned Mr. Hatchett and asked him to call. He came the same afternoon.

"What a pity you took me off so soon," he said. "I told you he'd call again. What would you like me to do?"

"It's a pity," said Ronald, "that you didn't happen to be in Eleanor Gardens when the man came."

"Well, it was your decision, sir."

"No, I don't mean that," said Ronald. "When you first saw him you were here by a lucky coincidence. A pity there wasn't another one."

"Oh, I see, sir," said Mr. Hatchett. "It was just a bit of luck the first time."

"Was it?" said Ronald. "I think history repeated itself this morning."

"How d'you mean, sir?"

"Don't you know?"

"Not till you tell me, sir."

"I think," said Ronald, "that by another lucky coincidence you were in Eleanor Gardens this morning when the man came. But naturally, as you weren't employed by me to do anything, you did nothing about it. But, as that might appear rather mean, you prefer to say that you weren't here at all."

"I don't know what you're talking about, sir."

"You do, Mr. Hatchett," said Ronald. "It was rather mean of you not to stop that chap, don't you think? But I quite agree. I deserved it. I wasn't paying you. So you've taught me two lessons. First, not to call off your instructions too soon and, secondly, to agree to pay you by results."

"Are you suggesting that I was in the Gardens, saw the man put something in your letterbox and did nothing about it?"

"I was suggesting it."

"It's quite untrue," said Mr. Hatchett.

"Well, I suppose it is," said Ronald.

"I'm glad you agree, sir. Do you think perhaps an apology would be in place?"

"An apology? Most certainly. But not from me. From you, Mr. Hatchett. I personally saw you here this morning."

"Why not say so at once?" said Mr. Hatchett. "It would have saved a lot of time. As a matter of fact, I saw you too."

"Then why didn't you say so at once?"

"I wanted to know what you were going to say."

"Why?"

"Why?" repeated Mr. Hatchett. "Why? For a very simple reason. I cannot believe that an innocent man would play about as you have. In the first place you'd have gone to the police long ago. Secondly, you'd have had them waiting for me here now."

"How d'you know I haven't?"

"I'm not quite such a fool, Colonel Holbrook. There are no police here. I know it."

"Well, what is it you want? Why have you been sending these notes?"

"I don't agree that I have, but whoever did send them sent them as a warning. What could be sent to Number Eighteen could equally well be sent to Number Nineteen."

"And that's what's going to happen if I don't do something, I assume."

"Could be."

"And what is the something I'm expected to do?"

"That's left to you."

"Money, I suppose."

"I didn't say so."

"Ten guineas for the first day and five guineas a day after that. For how long?"

"That's up to you."

"Suppose I took your advice and went to the police?"

"You won't. It was bad advice."

"How am I to know whether your advice is good or bad?"

"Don't bother about my advice. Bother about the facts, Colonel Holbrook."

"What facts?" asked Ronald.

"You really want to hear? Then all right, you shall. But I should sit down if I were you. You're in for a nasty shock."

"I shall do what I like in my own house."

"Please yourself. You'd really like to hear the facts, would you?"

"I don't really mind," said Ronald.

"Don't you? See if you mind this. Three months before the murder—I said murder—you consulted Mr. Plumb and begged him to find some way to keep Jane Doughty away from you."

"How on earth d'you know that?" asked Ronald. He was so shattered by the statement that he could not refrain from asking the question.

"The answer to that is this," said Mr. Hatchett, and he patted his hip pocket. Ronald looked puzzled. Mr. Hatchett brought out a flask.

"It loosens tongues," he said. "I told you I did a lot of my work in pubs."

"Mr. Plumb never told you that."

"I didn't say he did. I'm sure he wouldn't dream of doing such a thing, though, as a matter of fact, I don't even know the man."

"Then how on earth?" asked Ronald.

"Mr. Plumb has a confidential clerk of long standing. Fortunately for him but unfortunately for you he likes his little drop. Well, why shouldn't he? He works long hours and doesn't get paid all that much. Has to get his relaxation somewhere. When he was younger no doubt it was his wife. But now it's the bottle. Not excessive, you know, but just enough to make him talk when he shouldn't. That's the place to find out things—a pub. Anything except racing tips, that is. Don't be too hard on the old boy. It's a great temptation to be able to say something which nobody knows. Here's an inquest about a poor girl who falls over a cliff. Odd, says he, very odd. What's odd, old man? Oh, I couldn't say. Have another, old man. And so on. You can see what's going to happen. So there we are. That's surprise number one. Want to hear the next?"

"Go on," said Ronald.

"Now, this really is a coincidence. Not like my being in Eleanor Gardens where we first met. That was *not* a coincidence. But why my friend and I should happen to be by Spike Point when you and your fiancée happened to be there, I just do not know. One of the freaks of fortune, I suppose."

"You weren't there. You're lying," said Ronald.

"Oh, no, I'm not. I know you looked around to see if anyone was there, but my friend and I were lying on the grass—just like you had been. And we saw what happened."

Ronald said nothing.

"I said that we saw what happened."

Ronald still said nothing.

"Don't you want to know what it was?"

"I said what happened at the inquest."

"Oh, no, you didn't. You told your story at the inquest, all right. But that was just your story, not what happened. What happened was what we saw. Don't you want to know what it was we saw?"

"I don't know what you're going to say you saw, but I know what happened."

"Perhaps you've forgotten. You went with the young lady to the edge. Then you pointed out to sea with your right hand and pushed her over with your left. Then you ran like the very dickens."

"That's the only thing that's true. You've just invented the rest to scare me into paying you."

"You're scared, all right, but there's no invention on my part."

"If you saw a murder take place, why didn't you go to the police?"

"We thought you'd prefer us to come to you. We don't like the police all that much, either. But if you want us to go to the police, we'll go. And where will that land you? In the dock."

"All right," said Ronald. "How much d'you want?"

"We'll say twenty pounds a week to begin with. You can always come along with a cash offer later and we'll consider it."

"All right," said Ronald. "Here's your twenty pounds. Now get out."

"Just a moment," said Mr. Hatchett. "If you talk like that I think we'll send a few letters to your friends and neighbors."

"What's the twenty pounds for then?"

"To stop us from going to the police. If you want to avoid our writing to other people, you must treat us decently. We're not going to be pushed around."

"Who's we?"

"My friend and I. Two witnesses, d'you see, to say you pushed her over and your own admission that you wanted to get rid of her. Quite a case, isn't it?"

"When will you call again?"

"Make it Mondays. But next Monday see what you could offer in the way of a lump sum. That'd save us both trouble."

18

The Trap

BEFORE MR. HATCHETT LEFT, Ronald had already made up his mind what he must do. He knew that, if he started to pay, the paying would never stop until he went to the police. The one thing which he had learned in the Army was O.C.C.P., initials which as a mnemonic he could never forget because a rather coarse phrase had been invented to help people to remember it. This phrase referred (quite untruly) to a supposed physical inadequacy on the part of Old Cheltonians. Why the inventor of the phrase had chosen Cheltenham rather than Clifton or Charterhouse or any other school beginning with C is not known. But it was a phrase you couldn't forget. O.C.C.P. in fact stood for: Object; Considerations affecting the attainment of the object; Courses open; Plan. The most important of all these matters was Object. Is your object to capture the hill or to kill the enemy which holds it? A plan for the first objective may be very different from that for the second. So, in ordinary life, if you make up your mind what your object is, it is far easier to decide what you are going to do. For example, is your object to assuage your injured pride or to keep on good terms with the fellow who has said or done something to hurt you? If it is the former, you write a sarcastic or aggressive letter to the Editor of *The Times Literary Supplement* or to your assailant himself or to the most suitable person. Something like this:

DEAR SCUDLEY-BROWN,

Your statement over the wireless about my book was mere abuse, not criticism. I imagine that the power that you have to hurt and disparage people has gone to your head. When you are older you may perhaps realize the responsibilities of a critic, but I doubt it. I do not regret that I shall be unable to lunch with you as arranged on Thursday. I have no other engagement but I prefer my own company.

Yours etc.

On the other hand, if your object is to keep on good terms with the critic, however angry you may be, you either don't write at all and go to lunch on Thursday as arranged or you write a very different letter. If you don't write but just keep the lunch engagement, he will say, "I'm afraid I was a bit hard on you the other day" and you will reply. "On consideration I'm not sure that you were. I must admit I was a little hurt at first but after an hour or so I realized that you were right and I was wrong. I'm most grateful. This claret is really delicious. May I know what it is?" If you write a letter, stifling your justifiable anger and holding back the tears, you will say something like this:

DEAR SCUDLEY-BROWN,

I don't suppose you often get friendly letters from people whose work you have severely criticized, so I hope you will be pleased to hear that, though I squirmed under your brilliant literary lash, I realized only too well how well deserved the punishment was. If only I could have consulted you before the book went off the rails and, as you so rightly put it, "down the embankment and into the mill stream," I might have been able to save it. Thank you for the lesson. I very much look forward to thanking you in person on Thursday, but I thought you might like to know my reactions before then.

Yours etc.

As you seal up the letter you repeat for at least the third time the strong expletives which you have been using ever since the broadcast. And as you post it you probably make a rude gesture.

In each of these cases you will have achieved your object. The vital thing is to know what it is.

Ronald knew what his main object was, but before going to the police he decided to call on one of the barristers in Eleanor Gardens. He could see that his hope of avoiding court proceedings was rapidly fading. But he ought to have professional advice before he started the ball rolling. Otherwise he might unwittingly put it in his own goal.

That evening Ronald called on Ernest Myrtle. He had been at the bar for over twenty years and was experienced in both criminal and civil matters. He and Ernest were on very good terms, though they were not close personal friends.

"It's good of you to see me, Ernest, when you've just come back from court. Hope it's not too much of a bore," began Ronald.

"Not a bit, my dear old boy. Only too delighted. Sherry or gin?"

Ronald accepted a glass of sherry.

"Now, what's the trouble?"

"It's terribly serious."

"I am sorry," said Myrtle. "You've been through a terrible lot. What can I do?"

"I just want to be sure I'm doing the right thing. Someone's trying to blackmail me."

"Blackmail? Surely not."

"I told you it was terribly serious. It's true."

"But you can't have done anything, old boy, to attract a blackmailer."

"Well, I haven't done anything, but, if I don't do something, I shall be blackmailed."

"I'm sure you're making too heavy weather of it. No one's ever blackmailed unless there's something black to be blackmailed for."

"Well, I'm an exception."

"Tell me."

"You'll understand that before I became engaged to Jane, I naturally had to think a lot about it owing to the difference in our ages."

"Of course."

"At first I thought it would be quite wrong from Jane's point of view and I told her so. But she wouldn't hear of it. She was rather headstrong, as you may possibly know. Well, it sounds awful putting it like this, but she insisted on marrying me."

"She was very young and infatuated."

"Exactly. Another reason why I should hold back. She'll get over it, I told myself, if she doesn't see me. So I planned to take myself off, put my house up for sale and started looking for another."

"I didn't hear of this."

"No, because I kept it very quiet to prevent Jane from hearing of it. Well, she did hear of it and raised absolute hell. I was terribly worried and consulted a solicitor as to what I could do—for the girl's own sake—to stop her from seeing me. He suggested all sorts of things—making her a ward of court, getting an injunction against her to stop her from seeing me, and so forth. But when I tried to talk it over with her she became so hysterical that I realized that, if I did any of the things which the solicitor advised, she might become very seriously ill, even commit suicide. So, in the end, I felt there was nothing else I could do and so I agreed to our engagement. I still thought it wrong, but it seemed the lesser of the two evils."

"Well, so far," said Myrtle, "you seem to have behaved most properly."

"Well, I couldn't see any alternative. Naturally, once I'd made the decision to marry her, I was very happy. I was devoted to the girl and felt sure we should be able to make a go of it."

"I'm sure you would have. What a tragedy for you. You know how I sympathize. But where does the blackmail come in?"

"I'll tell you. Some clerk in the solicitor's office drank a bit too much and after the inquest told a man in a pub that I'd wanted to get away from the girl only a short time before she was killed. That was true to the extent I've mentioned. But, if anyone didn't know the whole circumstances, it might look odd to learn that I wanted to get rid of the girl only a very short time before she falls off a cliff while I'm with her. Suspicious people might think the worst."

"I daresay, but that will always happen. Anyone who knew the facts would realize that the suggestion was nonsense."

"I hope you're right."

"I know I am. If that's all you're worried about, tell the fellow to go to hell."

"Even though he's demanded money?"

"Well, if he came again, you'd have to go to the police. But, if he just tries it once, personally I'd do nothing. And for two very good reasons. First, it'd be most unpleasant to be involved in court proceedings. Blackmail is always news and your name would be splashed all over the papers. Unless they landed people on the moon when the story broke. Then, if Chelsea beat Fulham by twenty goals to nineteen, you might be squeezed out altogether. But given a normal day with the normal news, nothing outstanding, you'd get FIP treatment. F stands for 'fairly.' You wouldn't be referred to as Mr. X, because that always looks as though you'd done something and someone always learns who Mr. X is. I bet we'd know around here, all right. So, if it were me, and he doesn't come again, I'd forget it."

"Well, I'm almost certain he will come again. But there's a further thing I haven't told you. This fellow says that he was present when Jane fell and that he and a friend saw me push her over."

"Good God. This man's a real criminal. That does alter things. You're quite right. This is serious."

"D'you think the police will take his allegations seriously when coupled with my one-time anxiety to get away from Jane?"

"How can they? This man is a blackmailer. That's the first thing. Secondly, how can he explain not going to the police after he saw you push her over?"

"I asked him that and he said, first, that he didn't like the police and, secondly, in effect that he preferred to save it up and blackmail me."

"Well, that was frank at any rate, but who's going to believe it? Oh, no, the police will be all on your side. It's one of the crimes they really hate. They're hopelessly overworked at the moment and, if you've just got a case of housebreaking or fraud, they may not take all that interest. But blackmail is a very different kettle of fish. They'll be on this chap's tail at once."

"Suppose he never comes again? I've got his address."

"That's more awkward, because if the police simply confront him with your story, he'll deny it."

"I didn't tell you but he started off by sending anonymous letters all in print and cut out of newspapers or books."

"How many were there and what did they say?"

"There were four."

"Over what period?"

"About a fortnight. They said that I was a murderer and he'd seen me."

"How can you prove they came from him?"

"He admitted it."

"He can deny that too. You still *might* get a conviction, but what the police will do is to set a trap, and, if he comes again, they'll catch him. I should go straight along to them. You can never be sure when he'll arrive again and you don't want to miss him."

"I'm most grateful to you, Ernest."

"Not at all, old boy. It's a horrible thing to happen to anyone. Terribly bad luck. But this is a real criminal. Probably got previous convictions for this sort of thing. You may be able to pick him out from the photographs they'll show you."

"Well, I know his face well enough. But I suppose I'll get a lot of publicity."

"I'm afraid that is so. But you know the saying and it's very true: Those who know you will know you're the victim of bad luck, and those who don't know you don't matter."

"You mean that people who don't know me might suspect that the man's allegation was true?"

"Some people would suspect anyone."

"A pretty horrible thought that some people may be walking about the place thinking I'm a murderer."

"It's human nature, old boy. Some people suspect that every horse they back is pulled if it doesn't win. If someone falls off a cliff there'll always be someone to say or think that 'there's more in that than meets the eye.' I expect some people think that I've bribed the judge or the jury in cases I've won. So what? I doubt if there's any man or woman in the country who hasn't at one time or another been suspected by some person of doing something wrong."

"But murder!"

"You were involved in an accident. Just like thousands of people are every day on the roads. It's damned bad luck when it isn't their fault. But if a person's killed, there'll always be someone to say, at the least, that it was due to dangerous driving. And occasionally they'll say he did it deliberately. Don't think I'm not terribly sorry for you, old boy. I am. You've had the terrible bad luck, first, to be involved in a tragic accident which was in no way your fault and, secondly, to be pestered by a criminal. He might just have been a housebreaker or a thief but, unfortunately for you, he was a black-mailer. I'd still say leave it alone, if I possibly could, but your instinct was right. This is a police matter, whatever the consequences."

"Whatever the consequences?"

"Publicity and all that, I mean."

Ronald got up to go.

"Well, thanks very much," he said. "I'm most grateful. I'll go to the police in the morning."

"I should go tonight, old boy."

"Are you saying that because I didn't go as soon as I had the first letter? D'you think they may be suspicious of me because I didn't go to them at once?"

"Of course not. You wanted to see if the chap went on with it. What could the police have done with one printed letter? No, old boy, you've nothing to worry on that score. The reason I said go tonight was because of the chance that the chap may come again in the morning."

"Right," said Ronald. "Thank you again and I'll go there straightaway."

He walked to the police station and told the sergeant in charge who he was and what he'd come about.

"This is a CID matter," said the sergeant, "I'll see who's in."

Ten minutes later Ronald was telling his story to a very tired detective sergeant, who'd been about to go home to a very well-earned sleep.

"It would be me," he said complainingly to the sergeant. "I haven't been to bed before midnight once this week. My wife's beginning to wonder who I keep around the corner. All right, show the customer in."

In spite of his tiredness Detective Sergeant Simpson soon developed a keen interest in the case. He quite forgot about being sleepy. He even forgot about his wife and the little "bit" he didn't keep around the corner. As Ernest Myrtle had said, blackmail is one of the crimes which the police detest, and the light of battle was soon in the detective sergeant's eye as Ronald told his story.

"I'd like to get my hands on the fellow," he said. "But these fellows never resist arrest, unfortunately. They come much too quietly for my liking—that is, when you catch them. We'll go down to the Yard in the morning and see if you can pick him out. From what you say, I don't suppose this is his first job. Sounds a nasty piece of work. I don't mind burglars, even if they're a bit violent with their victims. But these slimy so-and-so's, they're like vampires. It's not so bad for you, sir, as you've nothing to fear. But the chaps I'm sorry for are the chaps who *have* got something to fear. Many of them daren't come to us, in case we charge them as well. We'll always overlook what we can when a man's being blackmailed. But some things you can't. Murder, for instance. Suppose you had pushed the girl over. How could you come here? Most people think it's better to be squeezed for life by a blackmailer than be put in prison for life. But it usually comes to it in the end. Their money gives out and then they either commit suicide or give themselves up. But what a terrible time they've had."

"It must be awful," said Ronald.

"Fortunately, this time he's picked on the wrong man. He must be a very stupid fellow or he wouldn't have tried it. What's the good of threatening a respectable person who's done nothing to be ashamed of? That is a bit odd, I must say."

"But he might think I wouldn't want the publicity."

"Publicity!" said the detective sergeant. "Unless you've done something wrong, publicity can't do you any real harm. It's a nuisance to some people, I know. But some people love it."

"Well, I don't."

"Of course not, sir. But he must have been a pretty dumb cluck to think he could get away with it. P'raps we shan't find he's a professional, after all. He may be an enthusiastic amateur. But stupid! All the same, his methods are very professional. The old gambit of pretending to help you and so on. Well, we shall see in the morning. And I hope we shall see the client before long. We'll have to rig up one of your rooms with microphones. When's he supposed to be coming again?"

"Next Monday."

"O.K. We shall be ready for him."

The next day Ronald and the detective sergeant went to Scotland Yard, but Ronald was unable to identify any of the photographs.

"Oh, well," said the detective sergeant, "perhaps he'd been lucky so far. But his luck is coming to an end."

On the following Monday the detective sergeant and a police detective installed themselves in Ronald's house and, having tested the microphone, waited in another room. Late that afternoon Mr. Hatchett arrived.

"Think I was never coming?" he asked.

"I didn't know," said Ronald. "Come in and sit down."

He took Mr. Hatchett into the sitting room. The tape recorder in the room where the police officers were listening was set in motion.

"What a lovely day!" said Mr. Hatchett. "I'm not sure that October isn't the best month."

"I take it that you didn't come here to discuss the weather," said Ronald.

"I'm only following the practice of high-powered American businessmen. They make a telephone call across the Atlantic at a pound or more a minute and always start to talk about the weather for at least ten shillings' worth. It shows that they don't have to worry about a pound or two. They're in no hurry. Nor am I."

"Well, I am," said Ronald.

"Relax," said Mr. Hatchett. "Relax, my dear sir. We play the game my way or not at all. If you'd prefer me just to go away, you've only to say so. I have no right to remain on your premises if you tell me to go."

Ronald said nothing.

"I take it your silence does not mean that you want me to go. I wouldn't dream of trespassing."

"Nauseating bastard," whispered the detective sergeant to the other officer. "The way they squeeze their victims. It's the power they love, not only the money. To have someone in their grip. I'd like to have him in mine. Let's hope he tries a getaway. But he won't. This type's too smooth. I'd like to rough him up a bit."

"Well," said Mr. Hatchett, "here we are on this lovely morning. What shall we talk about? It'd be nice on the cliffs by Westbourne today, I should think."

Ronald still said nothing.

"Tell me, Colonel Holbrook," went on Mr. Hatchett, "you were in a desperate state when you went to see Mr. Plumb. Why so?"

"I wasn't desperate."

"Not desperate? Not desperate to tell him that there must be something he could do to get rid of the young lady? Not desperate to want a court order to stop her from seeing you? Not desperate to want her sent to prison if she disobeyed the order?"

Ronald could not think of any appropriate answer. So he remained silent.

"You begged Mr. Plumb to tell you what you could do to get away from the girl or to get her away from you. It was even suggested that you should have a tape recorder hidden away so that the false allegations she was prepared to make against you could be shown to be false. You haven't got one installed now, by any chance?"

Ronald still said nothing.

"This girl had threatened to have a baby and say it was yours, hadn't she?"

Ronald did not answer.

Mr. Hatchett got up.

"It takes two to make a conversation. If you're not speaking, I'm going off. She had made that threat, hadn't she?"

"Yes," said Ronald.

"I'm not surprised you wanted to get away from her. But, instead of getting away from her, you got engaged to her and then most conveniently before the marriage she fell over a cliff."

"It was tragic, not convenient."

"It was tragic, all right. You pushed her."

"I did not," said Ronald.

"Then it was a very lucky coincidence for you that she fell. You'd raised heaven and earth to get rid of her. You take her to the edge of a cliff and she obligingly falls over."

"It was an accident," said Ronald. "She must have slipped."

"Slipped?" said Mr. Hatchett. "At the inquest you said she must have lost her balance and got dizzy. There was nothing slippery where she fell."

"All the same she may have slipped."

"Why didn't you say so at the inquest?"

"There isn't all that difference between slipping and overbalancing. All I know is that she fell over."

"Without any help from you?"

"Look here, Mr. Hatchett," said Ronald, "you haven't come here to discuss how Jane met her death."

"On the contrary," said Mr. Hatchett, "that's exactly why I have come here. You murdered that girl and I'm going to see you pay for it."

"You're out of your mind."

"Out of my mind! Perhaps it'll be your defense that you were out of yours."

"You threatened that, if I didn't pay you, you'd tell people that you and a friend of yours had seen me push the girl over."

"True enough. I did."

"And you arranged to come here today to collect some more money."

"True enough. I've already had twenty pounds. Here it is. All intact. Please count it."

He put the money on the table. Ronald left it there.

"What is your object?"

"I've told you. To bring your crime home to you. I pretended to blackmail you so that you'd be bound to go to the police. And no doubt they've listened to all this conversation. I bet they know a bit more of the truth now than when you went to them. Shall we have them in?"

Meanwhile the police officers in the next room were discussing what course to take.

"This is a rum do," said the detective sergeant. "It's the oddest I've ever had."

"Shall we go in now or what?" said his junior.

"Let's see if anything else happens first," said the sergeant.

"I think the time has now come for you to leave," said Ronald.

"Very well," said Mr. Hatchett, and got up.

"Who are you and what is your object?"

"You know both my name and my object."

"But why?"

"Because I don't like people getting away with murder."

"So you invented all that about seeing me push the girl."

"Yes and no. I didn't see you, but someone else did."

"Why didn't he come forward before?"

"Would you have preferred it that way? He'll come forward, all right, now. Now that we've got the evidence that you wanted the girl put out of the way. If he'd come forward before, there'd have just been his word against yours. Mr. Plumb had all the evidence of motive, but he couldn't give it. His hands were tied by the rules of the law."

"But this witness couldn't have known all that," said Ronald, "when he thought he saw me push the girl. He didn't know who I was or anything about me. He couldn't have refrained from going to the police in case there wasn't any evidence of motive."

"Maybe he did go to the police, and they held him up for a late run. But perhaps you don't understand racing parlance."

"Are you suggesting that the police deliberately withheld evidence at the inquest?"

"Sometimes they have to do things which aren't strictly regular. Sometimes they've been known to search people's houses without a search warrant or take them to the police station for questioning without arresting them."

"It's an outrageous thing to do."

"You'll be able to say so at your trial. No doubt your counsel will make a lot of it. But the charge would never have stuck if the evidence had been given then. Now, with this vital proof of motive, it will."

"Who are you? Are you a police officer?"

"Oh, gracious, no," said Mr. Hatchett. "That *would* be carrying things a bit far. No, I took an interest in your case early on, and I couldn't bear the thought of your getting away with it. Nor could Mr. Plumb, if you want to know. But there was nothing he could do. He was bound by the rules. But I'm not, Colonel Holbrook. Or, if I am, I've broken them. And with the greatest of pleasure. Now, how about having the officers in?"

There seemed no alternative, and Ronald fetched two rather embarrassed police officers.

"Well," said Mr. Hatchett, "d'you want me to make a statement? You've got it, as a matter of fact, on your recording machine, but I'll put it in writing. I'm officially informing you that this man is a murderer. Whether you arrest him now or later is a matter for you. Probably you'll want to see the other witness first. Or you may just hand it all over to the Westbourne police."

"Do you want to say anything, sir?" said the detective sergeant to Ronald. "I think perhaps I ought to warn you that anything you do say may be given in evidence if you are tried for murder."

"I'm not guilty," said Ronald. "It was an accident. I swear it was."

"You'll get a chance of doing any swearing when you're tried," said Mr. Hatchett. "Shall I come to the station with you?"

"Yes, please," said the detective sergeant.

"So you see, Colonel Holbrook, I am going with the police to the station, but not quite in the way you expected. Good day."

"Good day, sir," said the officers, and a moment later Ronald was left alone. He sat down in an armchair and looked blankly in front of him.

19

❊

The Judge's Advice

AFTER AN HOUR'S THOUGHT, Ronald telephoned Sir William Venables and asked if he could see him.

"Certainly, my dear boy, come over at once."

The judge opened the front door. He was bored and quite pleased to have a visitor.

"Come in, Ronald," he said. "Nice of you to come around. People don't drop in half as much as they used to. I suppose I'm becoming a bit of a bore. Talk too much about myself and they have to listen politely until I've finished. I do soften the blow, though, by giving them a drink. What'll you have?"

"A whiskey, if I may."

"Of course."

The judge got whiskey out of a cupboard, soda water out of another and a glass out of a third. It was all done with the slowness and deliberation of old age, and the suspense for Ronald was horrible.

"Or would you prefer water?"

Ronald would have preferred water, but could not bear the thought of any more time being wasted.

"Soda will be fine," he said.

He had to endure the preparation of the whiskey and soda, the offer of a cigarette, the choice of seats and a further deprecating reference to the judge's capacity for boring people.

"Of course I know that some of my stories must be interesting to people, but at the fifth or sixth time of hearing they can begin to pall, and so few people will admit that they've heard one tell it before. It would be so much better for both of us if they would. And then, of course, my sense of humor or fun reached its peak some thirty or forty years ago and today there are different standards. Try an old volume of *Punch*. Not only will you think few of the jokes funny, but many of them you won't understand. Well, I don't understand a good many which they print today, and some of my younger friends no doubt find puerile what I consider the side-splitting jape about Aunt Agatha."

Ronald did his best to listen without fidgeting too much, but it seemed hours before he found a gap in which he could insert: "I wonder if I might ask your advice about something."

"Of course, my dear boy. I wish more people came to me for it. People usually apologize for asking, but they can't realize how much pleasure it gives to me, and I suspect to most people whose opinions are sought. In my case it's not just the flattery, though that is always pleasant, but it's the feeling that I'm still able to do something which may possibly be of use to someone. The source of most happiness is achievement, however small. It's no doubt very pleasant to win a football pool. But nothing like so satisfying as doing something which *earns* a person half the money or even a good deal less. So here I am, my boy, at your service and very willing to serve."

"It's very good of you, judge. This is terribly serious, I'm afraid. In a sense my whole life is at stake."

"Your whole life? Perhaps it seems like that at the moment."

"You will judge whether I am exaggerating. You know that Jane was killed in a tragic accident."

"I can't tell you how I've felt for you."

"A man has come forward who says that there is a witness who will swear—"

Ronald hesitated. He found it very difficult to say the words to the judge. "Who will swear," he went on, after the pause, "that he saw me push Jane over the cliff."

"What rubbish," said the judge. "Don't let a couple of lunatics get you down."

"But it's more serious than that. The man says that the police held back the witness at the time of the inquest, because they had no evidence of motive."

"That was a grossly improper thing to do, but they'll never get any evidence of motive. I must say I sympathize with you that it should occur at all. And particularly after your terrible experience, and your present state of sadness, you must find it very hard to bear. But there's nothing to be disturbed about. Angry, yes. I am too. But there's no need to worry."

"You haven't heard everything yet, judge."

"What else is there?"

"I can explain what I'm going to tell you, but—but—they have got evidence of motive."

"I don't understand," said the judge. "I must have misheard. Did you say they have evidence of motive?"

"Yes."

"Evidence that you had reason for wanting your poor little fiancée to die? It's impossible."

"It's quite untrue, but there is evidence."

"You must explain."

Ronald then told the judge of his original interview with Mr. Plumb.

"At that time," he said, "I was very worried about Jane's feelings for me."

"Ronald," said the judge, "if you want my help, you must be quite frank with me. At the time you went to the solicitor, did you really want Jane out of your life forever?"

Ronald thought for a little time before he answered.

"In all the circumstances, I suppose I did. That's what looks so bad. One moment it's said I'm trying to get rid of the girl and the next moment she's dead."

"Of course, Mr. Plumb can't have told the police of this."

"No. But apparently his clerk told it to the man who came to see me. This man trapped me into thinking he was a blackmailer. So I got in the police. They hid in my house and laid on a microphone. He then trapped me into admitting why I'd gone to Mr. Plumb. So the police now have evidence from me that I *did* have a reason which, on the face of it, might make anyone think I wanted Jane out of the way. Then this man produces the witness who will say he saw me push her."

"That is the man whom the police kept back from giving evidence at the inquest?"

"Yes. The chap who came to me said that they kept him back because without any evidence of motive it would have been word against word as to whether I pushed her and, in view of that and the possibility of mistake by the witness, no jury would convict me. But now they have evidence of motive.

The judge thought for a little. "Yes, I'm afraid you're quite right, Ronald. This is serious. It was still very wrong of the police to have kept the witness back, but, if he went straight to the police after the incident and told them he saw you, as he thinks, push Jane over, there can be no criticism of him as a witness for not having given evidence before. The police can certainly be criticized and so they should be, but it won't alter the evidence. Of course, we don't know what sort of man this witness is. Or it may be a woman. And we don't know how far away from you he was. But, if he or she had good sight, was not too far away and went to the police immediately after the girl fell, there could be a formidable case against you. The coincidence that Jane fell when a short time before her death you had wanted her to be out of your life is bad enough. But the second coincidence, that someone who, one presumes, doesn't know you and has no grudge against you mistakenly thought he saw you push her over, is more difficult for a stranger to accept."

"A stranger?"

"A juryman. You see, I know you, Ronald, and I'm quite sure you couldn't have done a thing like that. But the jury won't know you."

"You keep on referring to the jury. You mean . . ."

"I'm afraid that, if this witness is reasonably reliable, I think they're bound to arrest you. A girl has been killed, you had a motive for wanting her out of the way, and a man is prepared to swear he saw you put her out of the way. On such evidence the police are bound to prosecute."

"So I'll be arrested and tried."

"I'm afraid so, if the witness is a reasonable one."

"It's pretty terrible not only to have lost Jane but to be tried for her murder."

"It certainly is. But I'm not saying for a moment that you'll be convicted. Much will depend upon exactly what the witness says he saw and where he was at the time. If there's the slightest possibility that he might be mistaken and you give your evidence well, as I'm sure you will, you'll almost certainly be acquitted. Even if the witness is a good witness and says he couldn't have been mistaken, there is still a fair chance that, if you give your evidence well, you'll be acquitted."

"But to be tried at all, judge, is a terrible thought. To be in the dock and to have to fight one's way out is too awful to contemplate. Is there anything I can do to prevent it? You just said that people who know me would know that I hadn't done it and—"

"Actually, Ronald," said the judge gently, "I said that *I* know you well enough to know you are innocent. I can't speak for everyone."

"But there must be others."

"Oh, of course, I'm sure all your real friends will think as I do."

"Isn't there some way by which I could get statements from you and them and stop a prosecution?"

"I will willingly give evidence in court of your good character and say, if I'm asked, that I do not believe for one moment that you committed this awful crime. But I cannot try to stifle a prosecution. If you were my brother or my son I would not do it."

"I wasn't suggesting it should be stifled. Just that I should go to the police or whoever it is decides the matter, explain my side of the case and that my friends believe me."

"Yes," said the judge, "you can certainly go to the police and make a statement and ask that it should be considered. But quite frankly I can't see what good it would do. I presume you told them you hadn't pushed the girl."

"Of course."

"Well, you've denied it. They know you're a respectable person and that you can call witnesses to say so. But they have the evidence of a possible motive and, if the witness the man talked about seems reliable, I don't see what else the police can do but charge you. If the Archbishop of Canterbury and the Lord Chief Justice of England both swore affidavits saying that they believe in your innocence, it couldn't make any difference."

"If I'm tried and acquitted, my life will be ruined."

"Not ruined, my boy. But I grant you it's a dreadful thing to happen to a man."

"Some people will always believe there was something in it."

"Not your friends."

"What about the man who sells me gasoline, the milkman, the postman and so on; what will they think?"

"People with nasty little minds think nasty little thoughts in their nasty little heads," said the judge, "but most people have nice little minds. You'd be surprised to know how many good people there are in the world. The crime rate certainly appears to have gone up and that is a matter which requires to be taken very seriously. All the same, for the thirty thousand people *in* prison at one time, there are fifty million outside. The percentage of regular criminals in the country is tiny. The percentage of people who ever commit a real crime—even once—is very small indeed."

"But gossip isn't a crime. Some of the nicest people indulge in tittle-tattle. 'See that chap. He wanted to get rid of a girl, so she fell off a cliff. Oh, he was acquitted, but I've always thought, No smoke without fire, you know.' "

The judge sighed. "We're all guilty to some extent, I know. But it's just one of those things you've got to accept, and I repeat, your real friends will stand by you. And what should you want with people who aren't your real friends? You'll always be welcome here."

"Even if I were convicted?"

"Don't be morbid, Ronald. Respectable innocent people are never convicted of serious crime."

"There must be exceptions."

"Well, I've never known one."

"Suppose I'm guilty but I was acquitted."

"Don't torture yourself with thoughts like that. If you were guilty I should sense it. Not because I was a judge. You might say, in spite of it. We have to judge on the evidence, not on hunches or feelings. But I believe that the ordinary man has a very fair idea of whether he's living next to a criminal. If you were acquitted but were really guilty, gradually you'd find that people had other engagements. Except me, that is. Because I'm a lawyer I'd still accept your innocence, even though I sensed your guilt. I'd stifle such a sense. And I assure you I'd jump hard on anyone who suggested you were guilty. But that's my legal training. We English lawyers say that a man is either innocent or guilty. And, if he's found not guilty, right, he's innocent. Other people have to be like that openly. But privately, if you were really guilty, they'd feel it. You'd have to change your name and go away. But what am I talking about? It's your fault, my boy, for asking those morbid questions."

The judge got up and put his hand on Ronald's shoulder.

"You and I have known each other for some years. Not intimately, but enough. I tell you quite definitely and with no qualification whatever that I believe you. You can't stop worrying till the thing's over, but the facts are serious enough. Don't twist them or invent them to make it worse for yourself."

"You're being very good to me, judge."

"You forget. I enjoy helping. I can't say that I've enjoyed hearing your dreadful story, but if I've been able to help at all or can do so in the future, I'll be pleased."

"I can't help being grateful, judge, and I am."

There was silence for a moment or two. Then Ronald asked, "Will I have to wait long?"

"Before arrest, you mean?"

"Yes."

"It depends how far ahead the police are with their inquiries. And I expect they'd refer this to the director. The Director of Public Prosecutions, I mean. I can't be sure. But they won't waste any time. A murder inquiry is always urgent. It could be only a day or two or it might be as long as three weeks. Not longer, I think."

"It's going to be a terrific shock to everyone."

"Yes," said the judge, "I'm afraid it will be."

"And it's certain to happen?"

"On what you've told me, it will certainly happen if the witness you mentioned seems reliable."

"Well, I'm most grateful, judge," said Ronald. "I suppose I ought to go and settle up my affairs, pay the milkman and all that, in case it happens tomorrow."

"Come again if I can help," said the judge, "and good luck."

20

Visiting

As Ronald walked home wondering whether he ought to make a tour of the neighbors and warn them in advance of what was likely to happen, he was suddenly startled by a hand coming down on his shoulder. My God, he thought to himself, so soon! He turned around sharply to see Melrose, the practical joker, smiling happily at him.

"By Jove," he said, "you responded to that one, all right. One of the best I've had. Extraordinary what a guilty conscience will do for a chap. You'd be amazed at the number of respectable people who think they've been rumbled at last. Income tax and all that, I expect. What's on your mind?"

"I'm likely to be charged with murder," said Ronald.

"Fine," said Melrose, "some people can't take a joke. D'you know, one or two have got quite angry when they found out it's only me. That's because of a guilty conscience, all right. Bye-bye, old boy. See you at the gallows."

And, before Ronald could make up his mind whether to explain, Melrose was on his way, highly pleased with his success.

After an almost sleepless night, Ronald decided that, if he was not arrested, he would spend the day and evening going around to tell people what was going to happen. For some he would have to wait till the evening. But Mrs. Vintage was usually about in the morning, and he tried her first.

"I wonder if I could see Mrs. Vintage for a few minutes?" he said to her housekeeper.

"She's just going out for a drive, but I'm sure she'd like to see you."

Mrs. Vintage insisted on Ronald getting in the car with her, and there they sat for almost half a minute with nothing said.

"Speak up, Ronald," said Mrs. Vintage. "I can't hear you. Bit deaf this morning."

Oh, God, thought Ronald. I can't yell everything at her with Dawkins sitting in the front. You can't shout out, "I'm going to be charged with murder." If we were moving he might be so startled he'd have an accident.

"Could I see you this evening?" he said eventually.

"Yes, of course. About seven."

"Thanks so much," said Ronald.

"Stop, Dawkins," said Mrs. Vintage. "I'm having half a dozen people to drinks," she added as Ronald got out. "So glad you can come. Drive, Dawkins."

And the car moved off.

Ronald wondered whether to tell Mr. Sinclair, and smiled rather ruefully at the thought that Mr. Sinclair's identification complex might possibly prompt him to take his place at the trial. On the whole he decided to leave Mr. Sinclair to find out.

The people about whom he worried most were Jane's parents. It was an awful thought to tell a father and mother that you were going to be charged with murdering their daughter. Such information simply could not be broken gently. However much he preceded it by explanation, the stark fact would remain. Should he write it instead? No, that would in a way be worse, as it would look as if he were deliberately avoiding them. Well, if he was going to have the ordeal of standing his trial, he ought to be able to go through these lesser ordeals. But were they lesser? It's true he would still be a free man, while at his trial he would be in custody. What a horrible thought. In custody. In prison. Should he run away? Go abroad? They'd probably have his name at all the ports already. And anyway they'd probably find him and extradite him. If that happened, his flight would provide further evidence of guilt. Eventually he made himself call on the Doughtys.

"I've got some rather bad news," he said by way of introduction.

"I'm sorry," said Marion. "Someone ill?"

"No, it's about me."

"Oh, I'm terribly sorry. You look so serious. What is it?"

"You won't believe it when I tell you. It sounds absolutely absurd. At least I hope you'll think so."

He stopped.

"Yes?" said Colonel Doughty.

"I just don't know how to tell you."

"What's it about? Have you done something silly? Don't be angry at my asking."

"No," said Ronald. "And I'm glad you asked. I've done nothing either silly or criminal—but it's going to be said that I did."

"A car accident or something?"

"It was an accident. I swear it was. But the police are going to say—they're going to say—oh, how on earth can I tell you? They're going to say that I pushed Jane over the cliff."

The Doughtys were so astounded that neither of them could speak at first. Eventually Marion said, "It can't be true."

"It isn't true, but they're going to say it. They're going to charge me with her murder."

"But who on earth—" began Colonel Doughty.

"I'll tell you what's happened," said Ronald.

First he told them about his going to Mr. Plumb, heavily emphasizing his anxiety for Jane's sake. Then he went on about the apparent blackmailer and what he had said about the witness.

"But if you never did this," said the colonel, "no one can say that you did. Who is this witness?"

"I don't know yet. But the police withheld his evidence at the inquest."

"But why should anyone say such a thing?"

"Why?" said Ronald. "I suppose it was some trick of the imagination."

"But you were lying on the ground ten yards away when she fell. How can anyone imagine that you pushed her?"

"You don't think I did?"

"Of course not," said the colonel, "but why should a perfect stranger *think* you did? You haven't any enemies, I'm sure. So it must have been someone without an ax to grind. Why on earth should he say such a thing? He must be mad."

"Of course, it might be someone who wants publicity. Sometimes people confess to crimes they've never committed just to get their names into the papers. Much safer to say you saw someone else commit a crime."

"That's probably what it is," said Colonel Doughty. "But surely the police would realize that when they talked to him."

"The truth is," said Ronald, "that it's such an easy thing to say. Very difficult, I should think, to trip a man up over such a simple story."

"Poor Ronnie," said Marion. "I'm so terribly sorry."

"You give me your word you didn't do this, Ronnie?" asked the colonel.

"Of course. How could I? I loved Jane. Why should I? At first I was very doubtful if I was doing the right thing in agreeing to marry her. So were both of you. But, once it was decided on, we were as happy as we could be."

"We'll stand by you, Ronnie," said Colonel Doughty.

Ronald next called on Nicholas Shannon. "Nice to see you, Ronald. What can I do for you?" Ronald had thought that, while he was about it, he might sound Shannon as to the best counsel to employ at his trial. He decided to open the conversation that way.

"Who would you say was the best man to defend a person on a murder charge?"

"What's wrong with me?"

"Apart from you."

"Why apart from me?"

"Well, I gather you don't much like defending friends."

"If they'll pay enough, why not? No, you're quite right, not on a serious charge. One shouldn't be personally involved. One wants to get the fellow off, of course, but one mustn't mind if one doesn't. And one would in the case of a friend. But which of my friends is about to be charged with murder? Not you, I suppose?"

"Yes, me," said Ronald.

"You're joking."

"Unfortunately not. I'm completely innocent, but I'm going to be charged with Jane's murder."

"Good God!"

Ronald explained what had happened.

"How dreadful for you. Have you told Myrtle yet? Whether or not he's a friend of yours—I oughtn't to say this, I know, but where the stakes are so large I'd feel I'd be letting you down if I didn't—don't have him at any price. To begin with, he's a hopeless lawyer. Then he always puts the judge's back up and, between you and me, he's pretty hopeless with a jury. He doesn't actually stutter, but he gets his sentences all mixed. One starts before the other's finished and so on. I'd never say a thing like that in the normal way. Personally I like him very much, but he'd have done better as an accountant. Don't tell a soul I said this."

"Of course not," said Ronald. "Who should I go to, d'you think?"

"One of two men. Dillon or Mountjoy. They're both very sound and good advocates. On the whole, if you can get him, I'd plump for Dillon but, if he can't do it, the other's damned good."

"I'm most grateful. Old Venables says that respectable innocent men are never convicted of serious crime. Would you agree with that?"

"Certainly. They're hardly ever even charged. If you've got previous convictions the police may think your handwriting is on a crime you didn't commit. And then, if you were committing another crime at the time, the true alibi may not be much good for you. So you raise a false one. It sounds like a false one and the jury say to themselves, 'If he's innocent, why does he put up a false alibi?' and so they convict. But that doesn't happen with a man of good character. The police don't know his handwriting, anyway. So they need real evidence against him. No, I agree with the old boy one hundred percent. So you'll be all right. But jolly bad luck being charged at all. I wish I could do something to help. I tell you what: I'll organize a party to celebrate your acquittal."

"I wish I could be so certain. People say that a clear conscience should give one confidence. But, if a clear conscience doesn't prevent me from being charged with murder, why should it prevent me from being convicted? They wouldn't charge me unless they thought I was guilty. And, if they think so, why shouldn't the jury?"

"They don't have to feel sure of your guilt, only that there's enough evidence to justify a trial. A jury has to feel sure."

Ronald next called on Hazelgrove, the rich disappointed litigant.

"I can't give you long, old boy. I've got a board meeting tomorrow, and I haven't faked the accounts yet. Wouldn't tomorrow do as well?"

"I'm afraid not," said Ronald. "I mightn't be here."

"Well, fire ahead."

"I wanted to warn you in advance so that you wouldn't get a shock."

"I can't be shocked," said Hazelgrove. "The House of Lords' decision in my case cured me of being shocked once and for all. Forgive me a moment. I must just look at these minutes. Go on telling me. I can listen all right."

"Well, you know about Jane being killed. The police are going to charge me with her murder."

Ronald stopped. After a moment or so, Hazelgrove said, "Go on, old boy. I'm listening."

"You aren't," said Ronald.

Hazelgrove continued with his minutes.

"It's a pretty serious matter," said Ronald.

"Quite, quite," said Hazelgrove.

"George," said Ronald, "I think I'll wait till you've finished with your minutes."

After about a minute Hazelgrove noticed the silence. "Go on, go on," he said.

Ronald said nothing.

Slightly irritated by the silence, Hazelgrove said without looking up, "Look here, old boy, I know some people say that you can't concentrate on one thing and listen to another. Some people can't,

I know, but I'm one of the exceptions. You see, here I am talking to you quite freely and at the same time concentrating on these minutes."

Ronald said in a raised voice, "Damn your bloody minutes."

Hazelgrove looked up. "There's no need to shout," he said. "I can hear you perfectly in your normal voice."

"You hear a noise," said Ronald, "but you have no idea what's being said."

Hazelgrove went back to his minutes. "I took in what you said perfectly," he said.

"You took in damn-all," said Ronald. "I told you that I was going to be charged with murder and you went on with your bloody minutes as though I'd said it was a nice day."

"Yes, it is very nice," began Hazelgrove, and then looked up. "What did you say?" he asked.

"You tell me," said Ronald. "You were listening."

"I must have misheard. Don't make a game of it, old boy. I'm busy, you can see."

"I said I was going to be charged with murder."

"No!"

"Yes."

"You mean manslaughter—a collision or something."

"I mean murder. I'm absolutely innocent, but I'm going to be charged with pushing poor little Jane over the cliff."

"But that's all over. The inquest's been held and it was quite plain it was an accident. The jury said so. They couldn't have said anything else. What on earth are you talking about?"

"A coroner's verdict isn't final. You can always be prosecuted later if there's enough evidence against you."

"But it was a pure accident."

"I know, but the police have got a witness to say I pushed her."

"It's these damned lawyers," said Hazelgrove. "They haven't enough to do, so they stir something up. I'm terribly sorry about this, Ronald, but of course you'll get off. The whole thing's a monstrous mistake. I've no doubt."

"Well, it is, but I felt I ought to warn my friends so that my arrest doesn't come as too much of a shock."

"Well, thanks for telling me. But I still can't quite believe it.

Except that after my experiences, I'd believe anything of the law. They didn't send me to prison but they pretty well ruined me. Shakespeare was right: 'First thing we do, let's kill all the lawyers.' Is there anything I can do to help?"

"I don't think so," said Ronald. "Just believe in me. That's all."

"Of course I will, old boy. It's a damned shame it ever happened."

Finally Ronald called on the vicar.

"I'm glad you've come," he said. "I've been worrying about you. A chap in your position needs a regular job. Something to take your mind off your loss. It's a curious thing but, however sad a person may be, he cannot concentrate on some problem and think of the reason for his sadness at the same time. You could not seriously work out a chess problem and think of Jane at the same time. I'm sure you make good use of some of your time, but you haven't got a regular job to compel you to take your mind off Jane's death. Believe me, I'm not suggesting you shouldn't think of her. Only that you should have times when you can't. If you don't mind my saying so, you need a counterirritant."

"I've got one," said Ronald.

"Well, I'm very glad to hear it," said the vicar.

"I'm going to be charged with Jane's murder."

"What!"

"I'm going to be charged with her murder."

"You're not serious."

"Unfortunately I am. I'll explain."

Ronald told the vicar something of what had happened.

"But who can this man be? He must be either pretty simple or abnormal not to have come forward at once."

"They say he did and that the police suppressed his evidence."

"But why should they want to?"

"Heaven knows," said Ronald. "But I've seen the judge and he says that, if this witness is reliable, I'm certain to be charged with the murder. It's my consulting Plumb that's done it. I'm sure you'll understand why I consulted him. Jane's own parents were against the marriage at first."

"Of course I understand. But it seems so unfair to you. I suppose they know what they're at."

"You do believe I'm innocent?" asked Ronald.

"Of course," said the vicar. "I can't think of anyone less likely than you to do a thing like that. It could only be a very evil person who would do a thing like that. And you're certainly not very evil—or, indeed, evil at all."

"D'you have to be evil all through to commit murder?" asked Ronald.

"Oh, of course not. There can be plenty of cases where there's some provocation or some moral excuse. But to push over a cliff a girl of seventeen who was engaged to you—well, it's an un-Christian thing to say, but he's not the sort of chap I'd want in my house."

"Then if I were convicted, you wouldn't want me?"

The vicar thought for a few seconds. "No, Ronald, I don't think I should. I'd have to reassess my feelings toward you and I suspect they'd undergo a violent change."

"Well, don't worry, vicar. If I were convicted I'd be away for very many years."

"Anyway, you're not going to be convicted. Why, you haven't been charged yet. But I'm terribly sorry about it all. If I can be of any help, let me know. What a terrible tragedy it all is."

"You do believe in me, vicar?"

"I do. I certainly do."

21

Completion

THE VICAR WAS RIGHT IN SAYING that while you were concentrating on one thing you cannot think of another. As long as Ronald was concentrating on calling on his friends and trying to assure himself of their support, he had less time for wondering about his arrest and trial. But, when he had finished his round, the worrying time began. How long would it be before they came for him? How long would it be before the trial? He had so often read that a week's remand was asked for on the day after a man was arrested. And so he would be in prison for a week. And then further remands. Further delays. Complaints by his counsel about the delays. Some cases seemed to go on and on before they came to trial. When an interesting or exciting case came before the public, his objection to the delays had been because he wanted to read about the case. He had never then thought of the poor devil in the dock who was produced once a week perhaps for a short time in court and then taken back for a long, long week in prison. How awful it would be, this waiting. And then eventually would come the trial. Would he make a good witness? How good would the man who said he

151

saw him be? How would the judge sum up? Ronald went through his trial over and over again. But he never allowed his imagination to dwell on the verdict. He daren't.

He started to take sleeping tablets as the days slowly went by. Surely it must be tomorrow, he would say to himself, but it never was. The judge had said he didn't think it could be more than three weeks. Three weeks! They were like three years. He thought of everything the judge had said. He was a wise man. Years of experience of people and cases. He knew. And he believed in him. This gave him great comfort, but the delay eventually proved more than he could bear. When the three weeks were up and nothing had happened for two days more, he called at the local police station and asked to see the CID sergeant. Of course he was out, and Ronald had to wait for the next day before he could see him. But at last he had an interview. The sergeant seemed cold and distant when he said, "Good afternoon. What can I do for you, Colonel Holbrook?"

"What can you do for me? What's happening about my case?"

"The blackmail, you mean?"

"Of course I don't. The charge against me."

"Oh, that."

The sergeant waited a moment and then said, "There isn't going to be any charge."

"Why didn't you tell me? I've been in an agony of suspense."

"I was going to tell you, sir, but we've been tremendously busy and I'm afraid I hadn't got round to it."

"It's disgraceful," said Ronald, "to keep a man wondering as you've kept me."

"As you say you're innocent, sir, I'd have thought your clear conscience would have made things easier for you."

"I shall report this matter to your superior."

"By all means, sir. The station sergeant will give you a pamphlet telling you how to complain."

"But what about this witness?" Ronald could not resist saying.

"Witness?"

"The one who was supposed to have seen me push the girl."

"Oh, him. There's no such person. I'm afraid our friend Mr. Hatchett was making that up to scare you. He was quite satisfied you'd murdered the girl and was determined to make you pay for it as far as he could."

"Why should he want to do that?"

"I suppose he didn't like to think anyone was getting away with murder. As a matter of fact, his name wasn't Hatchett and he didn't get the information from Mr. Plumb's clerk in the way that he said. He was Mr. Plumb's clerk. He knew all about your original interview and he couldn't believe that it was an accident. It was very wrong of him, of course. But he was retiring, so he decided to take any risk involved. The director is now considering whether he should be charged with causing a public mischief by misleading us into thinking the case against you could be proved. But I don't suppose they'll bring a case. These public-mischief cases are very difficult if there's only one person concerned."

"Why didn't you come around and tell me all this days ago?"

"I've told you, we've been exceptionally busy."

"You think me guilty, I suppose."

"D'you really want me to answer that, sir?"

Ronald had to say he did.

"Well, yes, I do, sir."

"Why?"

"It wasn't just the evidence, sir, it was your whole behavior. Not just what you said, sir, but the way you reacted, the way you looked. You looked as though you'd done it, sir, and I believe you did. But of course, there's no evidence against you."

"D'you think that people can sense when a man is guilty?"

"I wouldn't know that, sir. Sensing is one thing. Seeing how the man reacts and what he says is another."

"Would you have anything to do with a murderer, sergeant? In your private life, I mean."

"That would depend on the murder, sir."

"This one."

"I ought to remind you, sir, that you say this was not a murder."

"Quite, but if I were wrong."

"It was a horrible thing to do, sir. I wouldn't want to have anything to do with the man."

"Of course, if he were innocent that would make all the difference."

"Naturally."

"Well, thank you, sergeant. I'll be going."

"Don't forget to get a copy of the pamphlet, sir."

"The pamphlet?"

"How to complain about the police, sir."

Ronald left the police station and walked home. One or two people waved to him, but he did not notice. He was thinking too hard. How nice people were. They had all been so kind. Particularly the judge. He remembered everything the judge had said. *Everything.* And, remembering everything, when he got home he went straight to the telephone and dialed a number.

"Is that you, Mr. Highcastle?"

"Speaking."

"This is Colonel Holbrook. I've decided to sell my house after all."

"Are you sure there's no chance of your changing your mind again, sir?"

"No," said Ronald, "there is no chance at all."

But the next house didn't work, nor the next, and Ronald was eventually driven to the sad conclusion that he must make the final move. But how? This time it must not only seem an easy solution but it must be one. To a man as lazy as Ronald, the solution to the problem of Jane had seemed at the time to require a minimum of effort. Just a push and it was all over. But he had not realized that he would have to live with the man who had done it. Now he must go too. But there must be no mistake. He had no firearms and it would involve effort to get a gun. To get drugs, he would have to go to a doctor and, anyway, he might be found too soon. Motorcars, though most efficient at killing people who did not want to be killed, would be sure to miss or would merely mangle him. There were even miraculous escapes for one or two of the people who jumped in front of trains. He drove to Westbourne.